THIS BOOK BELONGS TO

MY FAVOURITE POEM IS

ALPHABETICAL POETICAL

Steve Morley was born in Bradford in Yorkshire. He had a number of different jobs before becoming a trainee teacher. He reluctantly abandoned teaching training to become a champion chicken slaughterer for which he was given the nickname Claudius, because 'he murdered most foul'. After a short spell in uniform, with Bradford City Transport, he left for the bright lights of London to pursue a career as an actor, a profession that has intermittently entertained him for more than forty years.

For over a decade Steve played Sergeant Lamont in TV's ever popular *The Bill* (for which he also worked as a script writer); this was a part he was eternally grateful for as he appeared so infrequently no-one ever recognised him. But forget the world tours of great Shakespearean roles, forget the trip to Hollywood, forget even fighting Cybermen and being the vet in *Emmerdale*, Steve still regards his greatest claim to fame as winning an award for being the first man to appear nude on Irish radio.

In 2006 Steve was nominated for the national award of Teacher of the Year.

In 2010 *The Nutting Plays* and *The Farmhouse Plays* were nominated for a Company of Educators' Award.

In 2020 Steve retired from teaching at the City of London School for Girls where he had been Director of Drama for twenty years.

ALPHABETICAL POETICAL

by Steve Morley

Humorous verse for kids

ALPHABETICAL POETICAL

CONDITION OF SALE

ALL ENQUIRIES

mrsteve.morley@outlook.com

For Thalia and Theo…

…and with thanks to Jo Russell and Jenny Brown

Alphabetical Poetical
Theoretical

Alphabetical poetical,
For now it's theoretical
If I can write some poems for each letter.
To go from A to Zed
Might do things to my head,
But maybe by the end I'll be much better…

I'll really have to wait and see
If I can get past letter B,
Perhaps I will get stuck before the C.
But if I do not try
I won't get to letter Y,
Let alone the one Americans call Zee…

So let's give it a try,
Wish me luck, wave me goodbye,
Because if I don't start I'll never know.
I must swallow all my fears
Of this taking thirty years,
Alphabetical Poetical…

…here we go…

A

A

A is a letter that's very hard of hearing,
In fact, it's deaf, you really have to say.
For if you were to ask it, to tell you what it's
called,
The letter A will always answer, "Eh?"

~ ~ ~ ~ ~

Anyway...
(The never-ending poem)

I really like the words that rhyme,
I use them all the time.
I really like the taste of lime
But not when dipped in…
…anyway.

An Indian burn upon the arm
Can catch you unaware
And if it's done quite viciously
Can make you want to…
…anyway.

Henry the Eighth loved Anne Boleyn
But not when she was dead.
Because it's hard to love someone
If they don't have a…
…anyway.

Some dogs they like to wee on trees,
It stops them being glum.
Then they meet in the street and say,
"Please, may I sniff your..."

...anyway.

When you've eaten too much grub
You don't know what to do.
You only hope you're not in class
If you need a...

...anyway.

I had a dream the other day,
It really was quite rude.
I stood there on the stage at school
And I was in the...

...anyway.

My friend is jumping up and down,
Right there for all to see,
And we all know she needs to go
Outside to have a...

...anyway.

We were so hot in class today
While waiting for the bell,
But teacher said, "Please go away,
I cannot stand the..."

...anyway.

So don't forget that poetry
Is with us all the time
But it won't always work if you
Do not have a...

~ ~ ~ ~ ~

Almighty Bamboozle

Don't ever disturb the almighty Bamboozle
Because if you do you will certainly lose-le.
If he wakes up mad, he will give you a bruise-le,
So NEVER disturb the sleeping Bamboozle.

It's said now and then that the mighty Bamboozle
Is not quite all there with a few missing screws-le,
He's mad and he's bad, he sinks ships with their crews-le,
So NEVER disturb the napping Bamboozle.

Do not question why the almighty Bamboozle
Is blocking your way while he's having a snooze-le,
Just thank all the stars that there's just one Bamboozle
And NEVER disturb the snoring Bamboozle.

So don't ever think you might wake the Bamboozle
By playing some music or singing the Blues-le.
He'll bash you and mash you right to Timbuktuzle
So NEVER disturb,
No NEVER disturb,
Don't EVER, not EVER, no matter the weather,
Don't EVER disturb the almighty Bamboozle!

~ ~ ~ ~ ~

This space is left for those who wish to draw the
ALMIGHTY BAMBOOZLE

Absolutely Totally

Absolutely, totally,
Thoroughly through and through,
I understand that forty-two
Is twenty-one times two.

Absolutely, totally,
Thoroughly through and through,
I understand that G-N-U
Spells out the word gnu.

Absolutely, totally,
Thoroughly through and through,
I understand that trillions
Will never be a few.

Absolutely, totally,
Thoroughly through and through,
I understand that sailing ships
Will sink without a crew.

Absolutely, totally,
Thoroughly through and through,
I understand that red and green
Won't make the colour blue.

Absolutely, totally,
Thoroughly through and through,
I understand a liar can't
Promise something true.

Absolutely, totally,
Thoroughly through and through,
I understand there are some days
I do not have a clue.

Absolutely, totally,
Thoroughly through and through,
I understand that doing nowt
Will leave a lot to do.

Absolutely, totally,
Thoroughly through and through,
I understand that every day
I'm learning something new.

Absolutely, totally,
Thoroughly through and through,
I understand that I'm just me,
Thoroughly, through and through.

~ ~ ~ ~ ~

Asparrowgrass

The sparrow in the grass
Was looking for asparagus,
But little did he know
That many years ago,
The word asparagus
Was back then known as sparrow grass.

~ ~ ~ ~ ~

And in the Middle

SPICK is very tidy
And SPAN is very clean
To lend a hand they dust the AND
That sits there in between

SAFE plays all the music
SOUND is what he hears
Between them both there is an AND
Protecting both their ears

NULL is really nothing
VOID's another NULL
Between them both there sits an AND
Invisible and dull

KITH is a relative
Of his twin brother KIN
Conjoining them there is an AND
Who's relatively thin

Spick and span, safe and sound,
Null and void, kith and kin
Why do we have these pairs of words
That all mean the same thing?

~ ~ ~ ~ ~

Alphabetical Poetical Nonsensical

A

An arm of Arry A. Amstead,
Armed itself with arms.
Alas it's now arrested:
Arson on two farms.

B

A bus of bumbling bombardiers,
Blew up bubbly breath,
But were borne beneath black biers,
Bearing them in death.

C

A clutch of clucking cluckerers,
Clubbed a clicking clock
Clouted it with callipers,
Cluttered up its tock.

D

A dearth of devilish dervishes,
Duelled for a deuce,
Dumb to all deliverers,
Deafened to a truce.

E

An early evening Easter egg
Echoed each echo,
Even easy Eric Peg
Echoed echo-echo

F

A flight of fifty fousand fists,
Fought for forty furs,
Forty-five of them were fizzed,
Falling on all fours.

G

A gross of goosy gander geese,
Goosed themselves with gee,
Guzzled all the green goose grease,
Gurgling great glee.

H

A host of horny hantalopes
Hopped about with haste,
Hatching all their hairy hopes,
And hounding them to paste.

I

An impish, incey, inky itch,
Inched to Ingleflut,
Iced it is, inside a ditch,
'It there by a foot.

J

A Jewish gent called Jersey Joe,
Jumped and jived in juice,
Journeying from Jericho,
Joking on the loose.

K

A kaftan koat kalled Klarrabell,
Killed a kricket kat,
Katching him in Konstable,
Kalling out, 'Howzat!'

L

A laughing loon from Lowestoft,
Lunged at Leaping Lane,
Licking it and lopping oft,
Lumpy legs quite lame

M

A measly man from Manchester,
Munched a mutton mare,
Mincing it to minister
Mostly to my care.

N

A numbskull in a nighty,
Kneeled upon her knees.
No, nothing new, it's Nancy
Trying not to sneeze

O

An oafish oat-headed offal
'Omed in on O'Keefe,
Ogling now those 'orrable,
Ordinary teeth.

P

A positively purple pig,
Punched poor Peter Pan,
Packing him to Neverland,
Paused where he began.

Q

A quizzling quaky quakerer,
Quaked a quarter quart,
Quacking out, 'Quack-quack-er-er!
Quizzled by a wart.

R

A ragged rogue from round about,
Roared out in the rain,
Rioting his every shout,
Roasting up his brain.

S

A Score of several seasoned swine,
Sought the seven seas,
Sixty-six of them were slime,
Seething like Swiss cheese.

T

Two hundred tons of twee tee-pees,
Touring through the Trent,
Tracking all the territories,
Trouncing with-in-tent.

U

An 'undred urban umbrellas,
Underused and all,
'Uddled under some fellers,
Upping them to fall

V

A volish vamp from Varriseas,
Vied for vacuums vile,
Void to all their vacancies,
Vacant to their smile.

W

A wily wolf from Washerton,
Wailing out a whine,
Wolfing down the watcher's son,
Washing down with wine.

X

An execrable ex-exit,
Exited to Exe,
Excited so to vex it,
Executing flex.

Y

A yodelling yam of Yorkshire.
Yellow as a yolk,
Yicked and yucked to York sir,
Yelling at your joke.

Z

A zealous zoot from Zanzibar,
Zig-zagged to the zoo,
Zealot zipped to see Zebra,
Zounds what a to-do!

~ ~ ~ ~ ~

Anna Conda

Anna Conda is a wonderful girl,
As sweet as a new popped pea,
But you put my head in a terrible whirl,
When you said she'd a crush on me.

~ ~ ~ ~ ~

Alfonso Faylin

Alfonso Faylin found he was ailing,
So he went to the doctor's house.
Alfonso found the doctor wailing,
So he was treated by his spouse.

Alfonso Faylin then went out sailing,
That's how he earned his daily bread.
Alfonso took the spouse's kaolin,
And that's how he came to be dead.

~ ~ ~ ~ ~

B

B's

I really like the letter B,
I like the things it does,
I can't say *why* I like those things,
B's just give me a buzz.

~ ~ ~ ~ ~

Bob The Butcher

My old friend Bob the Butcher,
Is a most special guy,
And once he asked a favour,
To reach something on high.
Two bits of meat were gathered
Up there on a shelf,
And he could not go near them
(It's not good for his health).
But I had to turn him down,
This really special guy,
For when I'd thought about it,
The steaks were far too high.

~ ~ ~ ~ ~

Bananas

Bananas are a silly fruit
Which bend in a curious way
More like a boomerang than a flute
With a taste that's hard to say.
But try to throw one through the sky,
It won't fly back this way,
And if you want to give it a try,
It's a devilish thing to play.

~ ~ ~ ~ ~

Black Boomerang

Never throw a boomerang
If it is coloured black,
Especially at night for you'll
Not see it coming back.

~ ~ ~ ~ ~

Burp Song

(Readers are invited to create their own music to this song.)

My friend, when going to his job,
Stopped by the local shop,
To buy a great big bottle
Of fizzy, ginger pop.
And when at last he got to work
He took a massive slurp,
Then he went in the crowded lift
Where he began to burp.

The lift was full of office folk,
Who looked with some surprise,
At my old friend who thought it best
To use a neat disguise.
So he looked at the people there
And shouted, 'Sing along!'
And that's when he began to turn
His burps into a song.

CHORUS
Oh it was wrong
So very wrong
Turning his burps into a song
Within a lift
Burps in a lift
On oh so many levels it was wrong.

The first song that he burped to them
Made them look all about,
Considering that they might need
To turf this burpist out,
But the song was all about a
Very funny devil,
And well before they'd realised
They'd reached the second level.

CHORUS

The second song that he then burped
Had them all in stitches.
'Twas all about an arsonist
Who set fire to his breeches
The fire brigade they put him out
Making him quite porous
And as the third floor passed them by
They all burped the chorus

CHORUS

By the fourth floor the song he burped
Smelled of pickled herring.
The people there could not believe
What each nose was smelling.
But then he burped a song about
A glue that never sticks,
And well before they knew it, they
Had got to level six

CHORUS   .

The final song he burped to them
Concerned the girl next door,
This girl was rather desperate,
Cos she was very poor.
The song was oh so sad they wept
And never saw him go,
Leaving them all to go back down
Right to the bottom floor.

CHORUS, THEN CHORUS WITH ECHO
Oh it was wrong (Oh it was wrong)
So very wrong   (So very wrong)
Turning his burps into a song   (Into a song)
Within a lift (Within a lift)
Burps in a lift   (Burps in a lift)
(All together)   On oh so many levels it was wrong!

~ ~ ~ ~ ~

Bear Rings

I have a little circus act,
A company of bears.
We like to train throughout the Spring
When they have left their lairs.

In circles they all like to dance,
Around and round they go,
With spinning shapes and pirouettes,
A dizzy-making show.

But then I always lose them all,
I don't know where they go,
I'm always losing my bear rings,
That's why there is no show.

~ ~ ~ ~ ~

Bookie

A betting man had a speech defect
You only ever heard mumbles
He failed his job to quite an effect -
That's how the bookie crumbles.

~ ~ ~ ~ ~

Boxer

Dracula had a boxer,
You'd often see him out,
He'd work until exhausted,
He was out for the count.

~ ~ ~ ~ ~

Braces

I have to wear these braces
All around my wonky teeth
My friends all find it funny
As we walk across the heath.
I tell them they're not helping,
And they will build a schism,
If I have to put up with
Much more of their brace-ism.

~ ~ ~ ~ ~

Canoes

Canoes are very difficult,
They're boats made just for you.
Not for anyone else at all,
Certainly not for two.
They're very hard to row at first,
You could turn upside down,
And as they don't have any wheels,
They're very bad in town.
So if you find yourself in one,
I'll tell you what to do,
Canoes don't worry me at all,
'Cos I can row - canoe?

~ ~ ~ ~ ~

Claire

There was a young woman called Claire,
Whose face was all covered with hair.
When she went for a walk
The neighbours would talk,
Saying, "Look, there goes Paddington Bear!"

~ ~ ~ ~ ~

Clerihew

E. Clerihew Bentley
Went on to invent the
Verse form known as the clerihew.
Its fame began there – then it grew.

The clerihew is a verse form consisting of two rhyming couplets of
unequal length, the first line always being the name of a person.
There is another in this book, see if you can spot it.

~ ~ ~ ~ ~

Conundrum

When I was young, not that long ago,
I joined up to a marching band.
I would march along, with tune and song,
A conundrum safe in my hand.

Whatever it was, this conundrum,
I never ever did find out.
But its deafening sound was so loud,
If you heard it, you had to shout.

Upon one day, it just disappeared,
And I lost my conundrum friend.
Wherever it went, I'll never know,
A conundrum right to the end.

~ ~ ~ ~ ~

Cuddly Toys?

At first it was a polar bear,
Ba-Ba was his name,
And then there was a dinosaur,
Who I called Bronto-Brain.
Next to arrive was Daffy Duck,
Then there came a dog,
And after that arrived a goose,
Soon followed by a frog.

And when at last my birthday came,
More of them arrived,
Three birds, a teddy, and a horse,
Were wrapped and so supplied.
At Christmas came a carload,
Dozens of the things,
Squeaky ones and some that burp
And one that smiles and sings.

They're all placed on my bed at night,
Just for me to see
Them sitting there. But pretty soon,
There'll be no room for me.

~ ~ ~ ~ ~

Collie

My sheepdog is a collie
He's very old and hobbles.
He rests his belly
On plates of jelly
Then gets the collywobbles!

~ ~ ~ ~ ~

Catpee

I'd like to live in a castle,
Or maybe an old tepee,
But most of all I'd like to live
In a house called a *catpee*.
You might consider this silly
But I think that you should know
That catpee when it's said in French
Translates as the word *chateau*.

~ ~ ~ ~ ~

Cowboy Oh Boy

If a cowboy is a boy cow,
Then what's a tomboy, son?
If a tomboy is a boy cat
How come your sister's one?
Cowboy...?
...Tomboy...?
...boy, oh boy, oh boy.

~ ~ ~ ~ ~

Crossword

Have you ever had a crossword
With any of your friends?
You loudly shout and argue till
It's hard to make amends.

There's one friend who won't let me speak,
She just thinks she's the boss,
I have to write my answers down
To get a word across!

~ ~ ~ ~ ~

D

Diddle-Hey-Diddle

Diddle-hey-diddle,
The cat played her fiddle,
The spoon ran away with the dish.
"Oh, cow," said the moon,
"Jump over me soon,
And I'll grant your every wish."

So the cow took a run
From the spot she'd begun,
And she leapt right over the moon,
She came down as a steak
For the small boy to bake,
And to eat with the help of the spoon.

Then the boy made the wish,
As he finished his dish,
And he asked for a very long time,
Which would pass so that he
Never ever would be
In such a mixed-up nursery rhyme.

~ ~ ~ ~ ~

What nursery rhyme is this poem based on?

Déjà vu

Déjà vu is a feeling that you have already experienced something that is currently happening.

Déjà vu is the name
Of the verse I wish to write.
But I have this strange feeling,
I wrote it the other night.

~ ~ ~ ~ ~

Dingo

I used to know a dingo,
A very quiet dog,
Quite unlike his brother,
Who snored just like a hog.

He was a cleanly dingo,
A neat and tidy dog,
Quite unlike his mother,
Who wallowed in a bog.

He always bought you presents
A very generous dog,
Quite unlike his sister
Whose name was Selfish Mog.

He always did the washing up,
A very helpful dog,
Quite unlike his father,
As lazy as a frog.

I asked my friend the dingo,
This very quiet dog,
What made him be so peaceful,
As silent as the fog?

And do you know what he said...?

He said:
'Did you know that from a very early age
I desperately wanted to be a Hush Puppy,
and so, one day,
I just thought and thought and thought and
thought and thought and thought out loud so all
could hear me, until my brains were nearly raw
with all the effort and I was getting a terrible
pain in my tummy, and everybody was nearly
deaf with listening to me, until, at last…
…I just closed my mouth...
...and made the din go.'

~ ~ ~ ~ ~ ~

Debating

Debating is a wonderful thing,
You can get a lot out of it.
At school, I wished it to be my thing
But then I was talked out of it.

~ ~ ~ ~ ~

Dolorous

There was a young girl called Dolorous,
Whose skin was all holey and porous,
She was in a play,
And earned lots of pay,
By playing a sponge in the chorus.

~ ~ ~ ~ ~

Drone

I was once in a room, I was not alone,
But I sat with a man who, he said, flew a drone.
I'd love to be able to tell what he said
But whatever it was went right over my head.

~ ~ ~ ~ ~

Dolphin

I once made friends with a dolphin,
Down by a southern sea.
And we would play out in the bay,
Then he'd come home for tea.

We'd spend many hours together,
Among the waves we'd picked,
And through the day, within the bay,
Me and the dolphin clicked.

He asked if I would like to swim
With him on the seabed.
But I think I need that like I
Need a hole in the head!

~ ~ ~ ~ ~

Dublin

Dublin has always been Dublin,
And that's what I've called it since school,
But would it surprise you to know that,
Dublin is really Blackpool.
Now *Dub* in the Irish means black,
And *Lin* as you may know means pool,
Put them together and what do you see…?
Dublin is really Blackpool

~ ~ ~ ~ ~

Dear Old Doggerel

Surely you've met the Doggerel?
He looks like a bloated froggerel.
He lives within the smoggerel,
And feeds on fermented groggerel.
Whene'er you're in the boggerel,
Be sure to look for the Doggerel.
He'll serve you sweet egg-noggerel,
So be kind to the dear old Doggerel

~ ~ ~ ~ ~

E

Earwigs

Earwigs are so stupid,
A silly matching pair.
They stop your earwax getting out,
But cover your ears with hair.
Earwigs bamboozle me,
I cannot make them out.
If they're worn in conversation,
The people have to shout.

Earwigs astonish me,
They really are a riddle.
How can you ever hope to part
An earwig down the middle?
Earwigs are confusing,
Their prospects are quite grim,
How can you ever see to know,
If one's needing a trim.

Earwigs bedazzle me,
They really hurt my head.
Wouldn't it be more sensible,
To wear a nosewig instead?
Nosewigs do enthral me,
They put me at my ease.
They'd stop the germs from spreading,
After a great big sneeze.

Nosewigs do amuse me,
A wig upon your conk!
And nobody will ever know

It was you who gave that honk!
But earwigs are useless,
Like rubber garden shears.
So why do we need wigs at all,
Especially on our ears?

*P.S. There is a song about a particular earwig who was
called Oh.
You may remember it. It goes like this:*

Earwig Oh, Earwig Oh, Earwig Oh,
Earwig Oh, Earwig Oh, Earwig O-Oh,
Earwig Oh, Earwig Oh, Earwig Oh,
Earwig O-Oh, Earwig Oh...
And so on...

~ ~ ~ ~ ~

Eating Caterpillars

I have recently been eating
Quite a lot of caterpillars,
All because those caterpillars are quite yummy.
I would like to tell the whole world
Of my taste for caterpillars,
But sadly, I have butterflies in my tummy.

~ ~ ~ ~ ~

Echo

I say *I say*

I say

Stop repeating what I say,

stop it *stop it*

stop it

I want you to stop it.

and then *and then*

and then

I'm going to count to ten and then

cop it *cop it*

cop it

You're really going to cop it...

one *one*

One...

two *two*

Two...

three *three*

Three...

four *four*

Four...

five *fiEe*

Five...

six *six*

Six...

seven *seven*

Seven...

...eight...

Eight...

...nine...

Nine...

Okay!

T...

~ ~ ~ ~ ~

38

Easy-Peasy

Sailing is a lovely thing
Though it can make you queasy
But when at last you get it right
It's oh so easy-peasy

Gliding is a graceful thing
Especially when it's breezy
But when at last you float on high
It feels so easy-peasy

Breathing is a natural thing
Though not if you are wheezy
But when you do it without thought
It's ever so easy-peasy

Cooking is a handy thing
That can be very greasy
But when your dishes turn out right
It seems so easy-peasy

Writing verse – now there's a thing
That can be very cheesy
But when it's right – it's sheer delight
Though rarely easy-peasy.

~ ~ ~ ~ ~

Eggs

There is a deliberate
mistake in this poem.
Can you spot it?
Answer at the back of
the book.

Eggs have no legs,
They can't run round,
They spend their lives
Upon the ground.
Eggs have no backs,
They cannot stretch
Aching muscles
Within their necks.
Eggs cannot swim,
Unlike kippers,
In the water,
They've no flippers
Eggs have no feet,
They stay in line,
When it comes to
Breakfast time
Eggs have no eyes
They cannot see
Me with soldiers,
Egg cup and tea.
So pity the egg,
When you dip its yolk,
Eggs cannot laugh,
And that's no joke!

~ ~ ~ ~ ~

Easy-Peasy (2)

If you pick up a peapod
And press it on the seam
Then hey diddle-diddle
It splits down the middle
Revealing the peas in between

~ ~ ~ ~ ~

Empty Banana

The banana belched!
Definitely belched!
And now I have to bin it!
Definitely belched!
Did so with a squelch!
And now there's nothing in it!

~ ~ ~ ~ ~

English Rule

In English, as you all well know,
There are certain rules,
Not one of which I ever got to know.
Apart from one, which I recall,
Went something like this:
'A double-negative is a no-no'.

~ ~ ~ ~ ~

Exit Signs

Who is it speaks of exit signs
        with any kind of passion?
Who is it said that exits signs
        would be the height of fashion?
Whoever looks at exit signs
        and wants to scream and shout
Is mad because those exit signs
        are all on the way out.

~ ~ ~ ~ ~

F

A Funny Girl Is Mary

Mary had a little lamb,
It grew up quite contrary,
But when it ate the other lambs,
Everyone blamed Mary.

Mary had a little goose,
Feathered not, but hairy,
But when it went and kicked the horse,
All around blamed Mary.

Mary had a little goat,
Dressed just like a fairy,
But when it vanished with a flash,
All the town blamed Mary.

Mary had a little gun,
She blasted all the prairie,
And when she threatened all the town,
No-one dared blamed Mary.

Mary's now a little lamb,
Not at all contrary,
But everyone around agrees,
A funny girl is Mary.

~ ~ ~ ~ ~

♭ **F**latfish ♭

Flatfish hit with a rolling pin,
Flatfish battered with a bat,
Flatfish can't sing sharp as a pin,
No wonder this fish is flat.

~ ~ ~ ~ ~

First Day At School

The first day that I went to school,
I didn't know a single rule
The other kids just had to tell me all.
"There is one person here," they'd say,
"You must look up to every day,
You'll meet him when we all go to the hall.

You'll know this person straight away,
And you must never disobey
Or you'll have nightmares when you go to bed.
He isn't big, he isn't small,
But you'll shiver if he should call,
He is the person who we all here dread!"

I stood before them, full of fear,
They took me to a door quite near,
"This dreadful monster lives in there," they said.
"He has no body, has no limbs,
He rests upon a chair and grins."
And then they told me that his name was…

….Head.

~ ~ ~ ~ ~

Fishes With the Dishes

There are fishes with the dishes,
How on earth did they get there?
They're in the sink, I cannot think,
They appeared out of thin air.

There are fishes washing dishes,
They just flick them with their tails.
I must confess, there'd be a mess,
If they'd not been fish but whales!

I'm so thankful for this tankful,
I could give them all a hug,
But I'll just sigh, and say goodbye,
After I pull out the plug.

~ ~ ~ ~ ~

Failed Poem

I'm going to write a poem
That will not have a rhyme,
But it will be a failure 'cos
I rhyme things all the time.

~ ~ ~ ~ ~

Forgetful Anteater

The anteater stopped in the jungle,
And paused as he tried to recall,
Just why he was in such a bungle,
What was he to do there at all?

Now was it for jam or for treacle,
That he had come out for this walk?
Or was it to meet up with people,
To speak of the weather and talk?

Or was it for getting of porridge,
Or just for a walk in the park?
He surely had lost all his knowledge,
Oh dear, what a silly aardvark.

The anteater thought as he grumbled,
And scratched with a foot at his pants,
And then he looked down and he mumbled,
And remembered the reason: Ants!

~ ~ ~ ~ ~

Friends

Daddy, there's a hippopotamus under the duvet.
Yes, I did, I told him,
But he said he liked it there.

Daddy, there's a brontosaurus under the pillow.
Yes, I did, I told him,
But he said it was warmer than the Ice Age.

Daddy, there's a rhinoceros in my pyjamas.
Yes, I did, I told him,
But he said that they really suited him.

Daddy, there's a duck-billed platypus in my slippers.
Yes, I did, I told him,
But he said they kept his beak warm.

Daddy, there's a thesaurus under the bed.
Yes, I did, I told him,
But he said he couldn't describe how nice it was.

Daddy, there's a polar bear up my jumper.
Yes, I did, I told him,
But he said it was just dark enough to hibernate.

Daddy…
Daddy, it's all right now, don't worry.
Yes you did, you told me not to be silly,
But I had a word with the hippopotamus
and the brontosaurus
and the rhinoceros

and the duck-billed platypus
and the thesaurus
and they said,
THEY'D SORT THE POLAR BEAR OUT!!!

~ ~ ~ ~ ~

Frog In The Throat

The frog in my throat leapt out one day
Onto the table where he did say,

"I am neither mouse, not rat nor stoat,
I'm a genuine frog in the throat.
I beg your pardon, but I must say,
I feel unwanted and in the way.
Nobody wants a frog in the throat,
So I will suggest we take a vote.
What stands before you is quite clear:
Would you like this frog to disappear?"

As to my answer, you might well guess,
I said, quite loudly, a great big, "Yes!"
But, as I said so, what did I hear?
My very own voice so loud and clear.
It was quite tuneful, so like a song,
And all because that frog was gone!

~ ~ ~ ~ ~

G

Galileo

Galileo made a telescope
To see the universe,
And what he saw when looking through
Put thinking in reverse.
Back in those days it was believed
The sun moved round the earth,
You could not think the other way
For all that you were worth.
But Galileo called it out,
The bosses called him in
And said that they would take his life,
He had committed sin.
He tried to argue his ideas,
But was broken-hearted,
And so the sun and earth both went
Back to where they started.

~ ~ ~ ~ ~

Get Up and Go

While lazing round the house one day
My mother said to me,
"Where's your get up and go, young man,
Where is your energy?

"You can't sit there all day," she said,
"It's lazy and it's wrong!"
But what if your get up and go
Has just got up and gone?

I looked at her in disbelief,
I knew just what she meant,
But what if your get up and go
Had just stood up and went?

She really was quite angry now,
And I would have copped it,
So I found my get up and go,
Jumped right up and hopped it!

~ ~ ~ ~ ~

Giraffe In The Bath

Giraffe, giraffe,
I think you're having a laugh,
You never seem to wash your neck
Whenever you take a bath.

Emu, emu,
What are we ever to do?
You never seem to fly away
Like all the other birds do.

Blue whales, blue whales,
You all have really big tails,
One day I'd like to swim with you
While telling you all my tales.

Wombat, wombat,
I never know where you're at.
If I should throw a Wom to you
You seem to have lost your bat.

Giraffe, Giraffe,
You're *really* having a laugh,
You smash the shower curtain down
Whenever you leave the bath!

~ ~ ~ ~ ~

Grandad's Snowball Spiders

"There's spiders inside us," my grandad once said,
"They eat our insides up, until we are dead."
"But how did they get there?" I wanted to know.
He answered, "They get there by hiding in snow.

When you make up snowballs and throw them around,
You pick all the snow up from off of the ground.
You have no idea what's hiding inside,
But spiders are clever and in snow they hide.

Then if a big snowball hits you with great pace,
The spiders shoots in through the holes in your face.
It crawls through your body like some sneaky mouse,
And into your stomach, where it sets up house.

And there it will eat you throughout every day,
Until you are so thin there's nothing to weigh."
My grandad, he told this, when I was a kid,
And from that day forward I watched what I did.

I never went outside with snowballs to fight,
I'd have to stay indoors, shaking with fright.
And so I stayed like this for many a year,
Frightened of spiders coming in through my ear.

Now I am grown up I see what was done,
My grandad was teasing, was just having fun.
But I am determined to get my own back,
(If he weren't an old man, I'd give him a smack).

I put snow in his tea, put snow in his shoes,
He picks up his paper, there's snow in the news.
And when to the toilet he finds he must go,
He sits and he finds it's all filled up with snow.

And as for the moral, I will now confide,
Don't scare kids with spiders eating their insides.
Revenge might well take years, but it's sure to come,
When you're on the toilet and freeze off your bum!

~ ~ ~ ~ ~

Girl With A Lithp

There wath a young girl with a lithp,
Who looked like a will of the withp,
When she floated higher,
She caught all on fire,
And tho she wath thinged to a crithp.

~ ~ ~ ~ ~

Grandad

My Grandad says, 'Don't pick your nose!'
I like that!
He picks his nose, in the car waiting at traffic lights.
It's true.

My Grandad says, 'Don't play with your food!'
I like that!
He plays with his, even if it is under his teeth.
It's true.

My Grandad says, 'You'll never grow up strong!'
I like that!
I'm not so weak I have to go to sleep on Sundays
after the pub.
It's true.

My Grandad says, 'You'll get square eyes!'
I like that!
I suppose he means like he has when he puts his
glasses on.
It's true.

My Grandad says, 'Go ask your Grandmother!'
I like that!
She says he never tells her about anything.
It's true.

My Grandad says, 'Speak when you're spoken to!'
I like that!
In that case how can I ask Grandmother anything?
It's true.

My Grandad says, 'You have to eat your greens!'
Oh, I really like that!
I suppose he means like he does at traffic lights.
It's true!

~ ~ ~ ~ ~

Garry The Biscuit

Garry wants his hair cut,
But doesn't want to risk it.
He thinks because he's very old
He'll end up like a biscuit.
I said, "Garry, it's perfectly safe,
Even though you are an oldie."
But he replied, "If they shave my head,
I'll be a Garry-baldi."

~ ~ ~ ~ ~

Giraffe in the Jam

Giraffe in the jam
What's he doing there?
Giraffe in the jam
It's really not fair
Giraffe in the jam
I won't get my share
Of the jam in the jar with giraffe sitting there

Penguin on the cake
He's doing a show
Penguin on the cake
I wish he would go
Penguin on the cake
But what's this? Oh no!
He's now eating the icing and learning to skate

Monkeys in the buns
They're playing a game
Monkeys in the buns
I don't know their name
Monkeys in the buns
They haven't a brain
They're all having a bunfight and I'll get the
blame!

~ ~ ~ ~ ~

Glue

Glue's not funny, it does not laugh,
When you've stuck your feet to the side of the bath.
Glue's not helpful, it does not aid,
When you've stuck your elbow to Gran's hearing aid.
Glue is stone deaf, can't hear a squeak.
When you've stuck your mouth up and you cannot speak.
Glue's preposterous, it won't assist,
When the toilet seat is stuck between your wrists.
Glue's not charming, it won't say please,
When you've got your head stuck right between your
knees.
Glue's alarming, gets everywhere,
Like when your bottom's all stuck up with your hair.
Glue is useless, it likes to state,
That we should stick together, but glue I HATE!

~ ~ ~ ~ ~

H

Hunger

There's lumps in the custard,
There's warts on the meat,
There's fire in the mustard,
There's nothing to eat.

There's string in spaghetti,
There's fur on the jam,
I'm not being petty,
I'm starving, I am!

There's bugs in the jelly,
There's mould on the cheese,
My poor aching belly,
I'm down on my knees.

There's dust in the corn flakes,
There's muck in the tea,
The eyes in the spuds
Are staring at me.

The bread's gone all mouldy,
The scones have run out,
Not one Garibaldi,
What's it all about?

The cakes have no Jaffa,
The tarts have no jam,
Can't find me a cracker
And no trace of ham.

No puff in the pastry,
No choc with the ice,
There's nothing that's tasty,
Nothing that's nice.

No rice with the pudding,
No fruit with the pie,
No sage with the stuffing,
I think I might die.

My sandwich is empty,
I haven't a sweet,
I've nothing to tempt me,
I've nothing to eat.

But what's this? A sparrow?
Twittering heaven!
Where's my bow and arrow?
I'm dining at seven!

~ ~ ~ ~ ~

Hero Me

I'd like to be a pop singer,
A hero in the charts.
I'd sing and croon and make girls swoon
And break a thousand hearts.

I'd like to be a footballer,
A hero on the pitch.
From pole to pole I'd score great goals
And end up filthy rich.

I'd like to be a film actor,
A hero on the set.
I would go far, the greatest star,
An Oscar I will get.

I'd like to be an astronaut,
A hero out in space,
I'd blast to bits those alien ships
And save the human race.

I'd like to be a scientist,
A hero in the lab,
I'd find the cures for plagues and sores,
A Nobel prize I'll grab.

I'd like to be a president,
A hero of world peace.
I would not pause to stop all wars
And make the fighting cease.

I'd like to be an activist,
A hero they'll not beat.
I'd save the trees then clean the seas,
And cool the planet's heat.

My mum says I'm the perfect kid,
A hero to a T,
She says no-one comes near her son,
And that's enough for me!

~ ~ ~ ~ ~

Humpty Dumpty

Humpty Dumpty sat in a tree,
Humpty Dumpty needed a wee.
All the king's horses said to the king's men,
Put up your umbrellas it's raining again.

~ ~ ~ ~ ~

Hercule

There was a young man called Hercule,
Who always did quite well in school.
A murder in History
To him was no mystery,
For Hercule was nobody's fool.

~ ~ ~ ~ ~

Hoarder

I'm going to have to stockpile
Some food for thirty days.
I'll keep it in the freezer,
No matter what mum says.

I'll be hoarding lots of ice-cream,
Raspberry sauce and fruit,
And maybe some milk chocolate bits,
(I do not care a hoot).

I wanted to do this quickly,
But now I'm not so sure,
For after a month of sundaes,
I'll not get through the door!

~ ~ ~ ~ ~

Horse

I met a horse the other day
Out looking for his voice,
He didn't often come this way
It seems he had no choice.
What can you say to such a nag
Who offers no recourse,
Except for you to tell and brag
You've met a hoarsey horse.

~ ~ ~ ~ ~

How Do You Solve the Problem of the Poet?

There is an old poet called Morley,
Whose brains always ache rather sorely.
He tries all the time
To find words that rhyme,
But he can't, and that makes him ill.

~ ~ ~ ~ ~

WHAT IS THE ANSWER TO THE QUESTION?

HOW WOULD YOU HELP THE OLD POET?

Hairs

I told my hairs the other day
That they were getting cut.
They answered me, "No chance, no way,
We're staying on your nut."

I took them to the barber's shop
At the end of the week,
As he began to cut and crop,
The hairs went squeak, squeak, squeak.

It really is a strain-ium,
When hairs upon your nut,
Refuse to leave your cranium,
And squeak whilst being cut

So now I have the longest hair
Of anyone at school,
It really is a cross to bear,
I really feel a fool.

My hairs are now tied in a tail,
They don't squeak or annoy,
But school friends tease me without fail,
Because I am a boy.

~ ~ ~ ~ ~

Hedge Hog

The hog is in the hedge,
He will not let the dog in it.
The dog keeps trying to get in
But the hog is always hogging it.

Dog gave the hog a gift
A dish with fresh fried frog in it.
He thought the hog might let him in
But the hog just went on hogging it.

Dog tried to get hog drunk
On pig swill with strong grog in it.
But hog just shouted, 'Bring me more!'
While dancing round and hogging it.

The dog went in the back
The hedge had got thick fog in it.
The blind dog circled back outside
While hog continued hogging it.

The dog attacked the hedge
He threw an old oak log at it.
Hog used it as a barricade
And now hog's *really* hogging it!

The barricade was large
The dog stared quite agog at it
He went away and left the hedge
And to this day hog's hogging it.

~ ~ ~ ~ ~

Island Wish

I'd like to be an island
Off the coast of Italy
My Grandad says, "That's all very well,
But don't you be Sicily"!

~ ~ ~ ~ ~

Ice Cream

The ice cream suddenly flew into the air,
Don't ask me why, it was just like a dream.
The ice cream suddenly splattered on my hair
Don't ask me how, but I didn't half scream.

Ice cream in the air and I scream,
Ice cream on my hair and I scream.
I scream, "Ice cream,"
"Ice cream," I scream.

Ice cream in my hair
Why wasn't it a dream?

~ ~ ~ ~ ~

I Cannot Get Up In The Morning

The bed is so warm,
    And I'm safe from harm,
        Outside a new day is dawning.
           It's out of my view,
             Whatever I do,
               I cannot get up in the morning.

I'm still half asleep,
    And dreaming of deep
        Beautiful things, oh so warming.
           I don't have to prove
             I'm able to move.
               I cannot get up in the morning.

I'm one sleepy head,
    Curled up in my bed,
        Don't care about winds outside storming,
           It's cosy in here,
             With nothing to fear,
               I cannot get up in the morning.

I don't, as a rule,
    Not once dream of school
        Subjects that I am on form in.
           It's better to dream,
             Of chocolate ice cream,
               I cannot get up in the morning.

Dreaming of such things,
    Alarm clock, it rings,
        It always explodes without warning.
           I throw it aside,
             'Neath duvet I'll hide.
               I cannot get up in the morning.

I go back to sleep,
    Like Little Bo Peep,
        Counting the sheep that are forming.
           I'll lie here all day,
                Much nicer this way,
                    I cannot get up in the morning.
It's warm and it's snug,
    Soft pillow to hug,
        The rest of the world I'm ignoring
           I'm one sleepy head,
                I do love my bed,
                    I cannot get up in the morning.

~ ~ ~ ~ ~

I'd Rather Like To Stick Around

The world is a story
We all play our part,
And we all know its history
Right from the start,
But I will miss this world
And all of its trends,
'Cos I'd rather like to stick around
Just to see how it ends

~ ~ ~ ~ ~

▎Used To Know

I used to know a hedgehog,
Who was known to all as Mikey,
And said he'd never wash his hair
Because it came out spikey.

I used to know a mammal,
Who was a seaside rotter,
And said he never went indoors
Because it made him otter.

I used to know a kangaroo,
Who was so very grumpy,
And said he never liked the dark
Because it made him jumpy.

I used to know a crocodile,
Who was so very happy,
But wildebeest he never liked
Because they made him snappy.

I used to know a rabbit,
Who was a little poppet,
But said she never liked being chased
Because she had to hop it.

I used to know a racehorse,
Who had a toothy grin,
And if he never brushed his teeth
He'd hardly ever win.

I used to know a teacher,
Who gave me lots to do,
And I thought if I got my way,
I'd flush him down the loo!

This teacher came right up to me,
And told me I was good,
Now if I ever get the chance
I tell the neighbourhood.

I now know lots of creatures,
They're all a bit like me,
Do you think that we will ever know
How silly we can be?

~ ~ ~ ~ ~

If I Were A Magnet

If I were a magnet
I'd be so interactive,
Then everyone I chance to meet
Would say I'm most attractive.

~ ~ ~ ~ ~

I Love Kids!

If you top kids with saucepan lids
You stop the steam from getting out.
Kids need to simmer in their juices
To show the world what they're about.

Some are tasty some are sickly
Some you tire of rather quickly
Some look gorgeous but turn out vile
Some look ugly until they smile.
Some are bitter some are salty
Marinated some are faulty
Some are luscious, some quite divine
You'll find some need more cooking time
Some are ready rather smartly
Some are hale and very hearty
Some are moreish some are less-ish
Some are best served cold with lettuce
Some need a wooden spoon to tease
While some, you think, just need more peas

But there's one thing I'm sure I know
With care this dish will grow and grow
Add extra love and less of hate
And when you serve upon the plate
Everyone will close their lids
And all as one say:

'I love kids!'

~ ~ ~ ~ ~

Igloos

Igloos are known as the Eskimo's sanctuary.
We have one in our house,
It's known as the lavatory.
Our toilet is freezing, as cold as can be,
You go for an ice flow instead of a wee.

~ ~ ~ ~ ~

Ironwhale

The whale looked at the submarine,
Then he dreamed an epic tale
Of an ocean superhero
With the name of Ironwhale.

Ironwhale swam through the oceans
Rescuing desperate sailors
And righting all the wrongs of those
Cruel, barbaric whalers.

The whale sang of great Ironwhale,
To other whales he'd shout it,
And then they all would swim away
For each of them to spout it.

So, whalers of the world be warned:
If you ever set sail – Oh!
You might well be torpedoed by
Ironwhale – Superhero!

~ ~ ~ ~ ~

J

Just Love Sweets!

I just love sweets!
They're really mega treats,
I like them so much better than roast beef.
Given my way
I'd eat them every day,
Making sure I always brush my teeth.

You can not beat,
A chocky or a sweet,
To chomp upon when watching your TV.
I do confess,
They really are the best.
And I'll munch sweets for all eternity!

~ ~ ~ ~ ~

Jazzy

Jazzy was a lovely kid
Who said that she loved verse,
But people said she must be mad
And sent her to the nurse.

The nurse took a good look at her,
She really took her time,
Then gave her a prescription
All written out in rhyme.

She took it to a chemist
(Confused inside her head),
The chemist read it all out loud,
And this is what it said:

"Give this kid a paint brush,
Some paint to stand the weather,
Then send her to a wall to write:
'POETRY FOREVER!'"

~ ~ ~ ~ ~

Jonathan Jilt

Jonathan Jilt hung from a kilt,
And swung from a sporran too,
The Scotsman in question
Had bad indigestion
So now he lives in the loo.

Christopher Katt murdered a rat,
And jumped on a fish as well,
Because of the slaughter
Of his only daughter
He lives in a prison cell.

Barnaby Budge ate all the fudge,
He ate all the curds and whey,
The swell in his belly
Began to get smelly
And so they took him away.

Christabelle Cake jumped in a lake,
And leapt off a bridge so high,
Because of her landings
And misunderstandings,
She's constantly in the sky.

Jonathan Jilt and Mister Katt,
Met Barnaby Budge and Cake,
And now willy-nilly,
They do things so silly,
They keep everyone awake.

~ ~ ~ ~ ~

Jippetty-Jappetty-Jumpetty

Jippetty-Jappetty-Jumpetty-jot,
He knows what I haven't got.
Jippetty-Jappetty-Jumpetty-joo,
He knows what you've not got too.

Jippetty-Jappetty-Jumpetty-jee,
He knows what's not owned by me.
Jippetty-Jappetty-Jumpetty-jell,
He knows what's not yours as well.

Jippetty-Jappetty-Jumpetty-jink,
He knows what I think I think.
Jippetty-Jappetty-Jumpetty-jo,
He knows what you think I know.

Jippetty-Jappetty-Jumpetty-jed,
He knows it's not what I said.
Jippetty-Jappetty-Jumpetty-jold,
He knows it's not what you told.

Jippetty-Jappetty-Jumpetty-jom,
Came to see where he came from,
Jippetty-Jappetty-Jumpetty-jay,
Found he'd left and gone away.

Jippetty-Jappetty-Jumpetty-jense,
He makes sense of all nonsense.
Jippetty-Jappetty-Jumpetty-jy,
Nonsense makes sense if you try.

~ ~ ~ ~ ~

Jan

There is a young poet called Jan,
Who makes verses up when she can.
And most of the time,
She gets them to rhyme,
But she finds it very difficult getting them to scan.

~ ~ ~ ~ ~

Jill

There was a young lady called Jill,
Who woke up to find she was ill,
She went to a quack,
Who made her lie back,
Before he presented his bill.

~ ~ ~ ~ ~

Johnny Pincher

Little Johnny Pincher rode into town
Riding on his bicycle upside down,
Mister Cake the baker, a corner came round,
Oops! Jam doughnuts all over town

~ ~ ~ ~ ~

Jack And Jill

Jack and Jill and a boy named Bill,
Were playing upon a rafter,
Bill fell on his head and was quite dead,
And the twins were filled with laughter.

Jack and Jill and a boy called Will,
Were cooking vegetable pies,
The food was off, and then, with a cough,
Will falls to the floor and he dies.

Jack and Jill and a girl named Lill,
Were playing at making bread,
The flour went whirl and so did the girl
And ground her until she was dead.

Jack and Jill and a boy named Phil,
Were playing at hide and seek,
Phil then hid away and to this day,
He hasn't been seen for a week.

Jack and Jill and a girl called Till,
Were whirling around and around,
The twins let go, Till fell in the snow,
And has never, not ever, been found.

Jack and Jill took some kids and a drill,
And made a terrible mess,
They were laid on coals and filled with holes,
And what happened next you can guess.

Jack and Jill went up the hill,
To fetch a pail of water,
Jill looked down, upon the town,
And shrieked at all the slaughter.

~ ~ ~ ~ ~

Jittery Jack

Jittery Jack had quite a knack
For falling on his back.
But as he walked the tightrope
He very soon got the sack.

~ ~ ~ ~ ~

K

Kakapo and Kiwi

The kakapo and kiwi birds
Went out one day for tea
Deciding then between themselves
To fly above the sea
But though they thought they'd planned it all
The future wasn't bright
For kakapo and kiwi birds
Are neither blessed with flight

~ ~ ~ ~ ~

Kelly

There was an old lady called Kelly,
Who became quite well known on the telly.
It wasn't the fact
She could sing or could act,
But because she was awfully smelly.

~ ~ ~ ~ ~

Kilometre

Could you ever kilometre?
I don't think that I could,
Because I think a metre holds
An awful lot of blood.

~ ~ ~ ~ ~

Ketteledrum

My kettledrum is famous,
A very well-known thing,
For when it's on the gas stove

It begins to sing.

My kettledrum is magic,
The finest you could see,
For when I bang upon it,
It makes a cup of tea

~ ~ ~ ~ ~

Kelvin and Melvin

There once was a young lad called Kelvin,
Whose one-legged brother was Melvin.
His hatred was such
That he'd kick Melvin's crutch,
And what else he did we won't delve in.

~ ~ ~ ~ ~

Kath

There was a young lady called Kath,
Who never would get in a bath,
Her father he pleaded,
Until she was seeded,
And planted beside the front path.

~ ~ ~ ~ ~

Kiss Bird

Whoever it was who made the bird,
Was so pleased he went to kiss its neck.
But then he stopped and thought awhile,
Before he gave the bird its peck.

~ ~ ~ ~ ~

Kit

There was a young lady called Kit,
Who found that she never could sit,
When she went to sit down,
She fell like a clown,
Which just wasn't funny, one bit!

~ ~ ~ ~ ~

Kollide-a-Scope

My father bought a telescope,
To see the Moon and Mars,
He swung it round, it hit his head,
And now he's seeing stars.

He staggered all about the room,
I asked him what he saw,
"Colliding with this scope," he said,
"I think has broke my jaw."

"I thought I'd bought a telescope,"
He said, and held his head,
"But now I see that I have a
Kollide-a-Scope instead."

~ ~ ~ ~ ~

L

Larry Dann

Mummy Dann, said to her young man,
I think I'll call you Garry.
But Larry Dann said to his Mam,
"I'm perfectly happy as Larry."

*'Happy as Larry' is a common expression originating in
Australia and thought to derive from the word 'larrikin', an
Australian term for an unruly young man.*

~ ~ ~ ~ ~

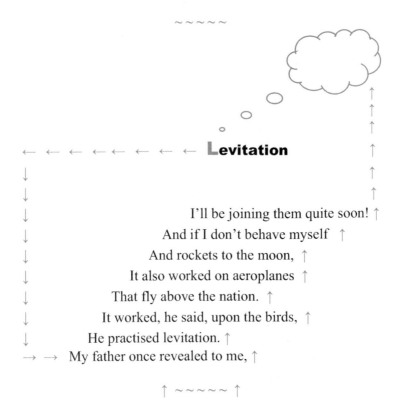

Levitation

I'll be joining them quite soon! ↑
And if I don't behave myself ↑
And rockets to the moon, ↑
It also worked on aeroplanes ↑
That fly above the nation. ↑
It worked, he said, upon the birds, ↑
He practised levitation. ↑
My father once revealed to me, ↑

↑ ~ ~ ~ ~ ~ ↑

Lucky

My friend Lucky has lost his leg,
He hops the streets and he tries to beg,
There's just one thing he hopes to do,
Find someone to buy his other shoe

My friend Lucky has lost his eye,
He only sees half the things pass by,
There's just one thing he hopes will pass,
Find some glasses with only one glass.

My friend Lucky has lost his arm,
Why he should, he never did no harm,
There's just one thing he wants for sure,
Find a man to teach him semaphore.

My friend Lucky has lost his nose,
Where it moved to nobody knows,
There's just one thing he wants like hell,
To find some flowers that he can smell.

My friend Lucky has lost his mind,
He hops the streets and he tries to find,
Leg, arm and nose and someone kind
To show him the man who made him blind.

How unkind for one so plucky,
To be saddled with a name...
                    ...the likes of...
                              ...Lucky.

~ ~ ~ ~ ~

Little Mary's Prayer

God in Heaven please listen,
I've not asked since You know when,
But do me this one favour,
And I will not ask again.

The first night could be awful,
My parents will both be there,
My Grandma will bring Grandad,
And really I do not care

If I mess up all my words,
And trample on Joseph's toes,
And bash into the shepherds
And tangle with Herod's clothes,

And trip up all the angels.
I do not care who sees us.
But dearest God in Heaven,
Don't let me drop Your Jesus.

~ ~ ~ ~ ~

Laughing Cavalier

What has he got to laugh about, that laughing Cavalier?
Did he just catch a Roundhead and kick him in the rear?
Or did King Charles just ring him up to take him for a beer?
Just what's he got to grin about, that laughing cavalier?

What has he got to smirk about, that laughing Cavalier?
Did he just take a Roundhead and make him quake in fear?
Or did the National Theatre say he's needed for King Lear?
Just what's he got to smile about, that laughing Cavalier?

Why does he seem to chortle so, that laughing Cavalier?
Did he just grab a Roundhead and smack him in the ear?
Or has he won a raffle worth a thousand pounds a year?
Just what's he got laugh about, that laughing Cavalier?

What has he creased his mug about, that laughing Cavalier?
Did he just see a Roundhead all dressed up in women's gear?
Or did he hear that Cromwell just fell down from Brighton
pier?
Oh what's he so damned smug about that laughing Cavalier?

~ ~ ~ ~ ~

Lance

My name is Lance.
It's a very unpopular name.
It's a name that seems to have been forgot.
Poor old Lance!
But back in King Arthur's times
Parents called their children Lance a lot.

~ ~ ~ ~ ~

Librarian

My old friend the librarian
Will ask the oddest things!
He bounced into my house one day
As if he walked on springs.
He spoke about the time of year,
He talked about his health,
But then he asked if he could have
My trousers for his shelf.
He wanted but a lower part,
The bottom of one leg,
And so I gave him what he asked,
'Twas strange to see him beg.
I asked him why he wanted it,
And with the strangest looks,
He said, of course, it was to be
A turn-up for the books.

~ ~ ~ ~ ~

Lazy Poet

My mum says I am lazy

                       I say I am not

To prove it I will take a

                       pencil and will jot

A verse about a lazy

                       poet which will prove

My mother wrong when I end

                       the poem

~ ~ ~ ~ ~

Let Us Talk About The Batman

Let us talk about the Batman
And the villains whom he fights,
As he ventures from the Bat Cave
In his Bat Cloak and his tights.

Now the Batman is a rich man,
Both his parents he saw killed,
And they left him lots of money
(Did they know what they had willed?).

So Bruce Wayne (that's his real name),
Thinks of vengeance all day long,
And goes looking for those killers
With desire to right the wrong.

And he dresses in the costume
Of a dark, bloodthirsty beast,
And wanders round the streets at night
(It's weird, to say the least).

And then he starts to prey upon
Some poor unsuspecting souls
Who dress up as cats and penguins
And reside in darkened holes.

If you or I ever saw them,
One fine day upon the street,
We'd say to them, "Come here my son,
There is someone you should meet."

And we'd take them to a doctor,
We would knock upon his door,
And say, "This person's ill, you know,
Can you please find him a cure?"

But the Batman does not do this,
He would rather hunt them down,
And terrify and torture them
And pursue them round the town.

The Batman, he is merciless,
He is bereft of pity,
He hunts them in his Batmobile
Throughout that Gotham City.

So do you think the Riddler,
Or Penguin, Joker or Cat,
Are really so much worse than a
Rich boy who thinks he's a bat?

~ ~ ~ ~ ~

M

My Brother Swallowed a Torch!

My brother swallowed a torch!
I had hidden it in his drink.
Such a silly thing to do,
Ridiculous, you must think.
I just stood and stared at him
As he drank and emptied the cup,
But it was really worth it
When the whole of his face lit up!

~ ~ ~ ~ ~

Max Morley

Max Morley once said to his Mummy,
"I'd love to blow air on your tummy!"
So he blew and he blew.
Till the raspberries grew,
Saying, "Mummy, your tummy is yummy!"

~ ~ ~ ~ ~

Maths

Learn your lessons if you've any sense,
    Like your English and also your French.
        Learn them all (like swimming in the baths),
            But most of all you must learn your maths.

Maths is useful, maths is really fun,
    Maths helps you do what needs to be done.
        Maths will stop you going truly mad,
            Maths will also show you how to add.

Maths will prevent you from getting sacked,
    By showing the boss you can subtract.
        Think of the things that you can now do,
            Like counting animals in the zoo.

Maths will feed you any time of day,
    Come let me show you my take-away.
        Counting the chips needed for the fry?
            Got some more people? Then multiply.

Maths will help you know how many times,
    Twos go into six and threes into nines.
        Maths will help you count all the toads,
            That run from the river down the roads.

Maths lets you count the legs of the bees,
    It's really cool cos it's the bees' knees!
        Maths will show you (it's easily done),
            How to count the bubbles in your gum.

Maths will say (it comes as no surprise),
    What will happen with your multiplies,
        Two times three equals eight less two,
BUT IF YOU HAVEN'T GOT A CALCULATOR..
            ...GOD BLESS YOU!

~ ~ ~ ~ ~

Mister McGrew

Mister McGrew went to the zoo
And because he was thin, they kept him in.
Yes, he was thin, he wasn't thick,
So they called him an insect and named him
Stick

~ ~ ~ ~ ~

Mona Lisa's Dad

Mona Lisa's dear old father
Said unto her one day,
"I've found you a decent job, dear,
You'll really like the pay.
It is posing for an artist,
He has your name on file,
But you'll never keep it, girl,
If you don't learn to smile."

~ ~ ~ ~ ~

My Mum's a Mess

My mum's a mess,
she's always in muddles,
except when I'm sad,
then she's dead good at cuddles.

My mum's a mess,
she's awful at cooking,
but that's not so bad,
cos nobody's looking.

My mum's a mess,
she's really untidy,
but we all help out
especially on Friday.

My mum's a mess,
her hair it's in rollers,
but then when they're out,
she's really quite gorgeous.

My mum's a mess,
she's doesn't like cleaning,
but then it's my fault,
there's jam on the ceiling.

My mum's a mess,
she's frightened by spiders,
she just doesn't want
them wriggling inside us.

My mum's a mess,
forgets like Bo-Peep,
but there's no-one else
can sing me to sleep.

~ ~ ~ ~ ~

Maths Tests

I do not mean to brag at all,
I do not mean to shout,
But how many maths tests I have failed,
I cannot even count.

~ ~ ~ ~ ~

Max

There was a young boy called Max,
Who never quite had all the facts,
He never quite knew,
If butterflies flew,
Or wiggled around on their backs

~ ~ ~ ~ ~

Mother's Ruin

Mother's really told me off,
She gave me quite a drubbing,
But how can I scrub behind my ears
When I can't see what I'm scrubbing?

Mother's had another go,
I've never heard such language,
But how can I grow up big and strong,
When she makes me eat boiled cabbage?

Mother's told me off again,
I've never had as many,
But how on earth do I pull up socks,
When I'm not wearing any?

Mother's shouting up the stairs,
In a voice that's doom and gloom,
But how will I not get very far,
If I don't clean my bedroom?

Mother's shouting out once more,
She's asking what I'm doing.
I'm sulking, because I don't know why
I'm going to be her ruin.

~ ~ ~ ~ ~

N

Noose

Any old goose can tell that a noose
Is made for things to hang in.
And any old snake can see at a shake,
It's not for placing fangs in.

Any old horse can see, why of course,
A noose is not for facing.
And any old goat can see that its throat
Is not a thing to place in.

Any old moose will say that a noose,
Is not a thing for fetching.
And any old goose will say that a noose,
Was what its neck got stretched in.

~ ~ ~ ~ ~

Nose

I looked at you…

        …as you picked your nose

I watched you…

        …where you sat

And I realised…

        …if I'd picked your nose

I'd have picked one…

        …better than that

~ ~ ~ ~ ~

Nelly The Elephant

Nelly the elephant packed her trunk
And said goodbye to the circus,
A rubber trumpet she had found
And played it oh, so grand,
And now she searches everywhere
To find a rubber band.

~ ~ ~ ~ ~

Nic

There was a young lady called Nic,
Who tended to speak rather quick,
And talk fast she could,
So none understood,
Which made them all think she was thick.

~ ~ ~ ~ ~

Not Last Night

Not last night but the night before,
A Grizzly knocked upon my door.
"Please sir, please sir," he growled at me,
"A dog sir, dog sir, did you see?"
"No sir, no sir," I said to he,
"Not by the skins of my old tee-pee."

Not last night but the night before,
A dog did knock upon my door.
"Woof, sir, woof sir," he barked and spat,
"But have you seen a bad Tom Cat?"
"No sir, no sir, and I must stress,
Not by the feathers on my headdress."

Not last night but one before that,
Door did knock and there stood a cat.
"Please sir, please sir," he hissed at me,
"Was a mouse looking out for me?"
"No cat, no cat," I said to Tom,
"Not by the bangs on my old war drum."

Not last night but two nights ago,
Came there a knocking soft and slow,
A mouse stood there and squeaked to me,
"Please can I hide in your tee-pee?"

"Yes mouse, yes mouse," I said, "of course,
"Hide behind the ears of my best horse."

Not tonight but the night before,
Knocks were loud upon my door.
There stood Grizzly, Dog and Cat,
Come to find where the mouse was at
"Here sirs, here," I said with a bow,
Then we began on a long pow-wow.

Not last night, nor the night before,
Tonight it is and on the floor,
Grizzly, Dog and Cat and Mouse,
Drink the health of all in the house.
Smiles all round, hostilities cease,
As they sit and smoke the pipe of peace.

~ ~ ~ ~ ~

Nobody's Fools (A Song)

(Readers are invited to create their own music for this song.)

Terry loves our Lucy,
Sue's in love with Biff,
Dennis doesn't love anyone at all,
Except perhaps Miss Smith.
Miss Smith is our teacher,
She rides a motorbike,
Sheila thinks it's dangerous,
And so does little Mike...Oh!

Chorus:

Singing a song about Class A Eleven,
Singing a song about the worst of schools,
We are the class of twenty-seven.
But we'll turn out nobody's fools.
*   (Clap-clap, clap)*
No, we'll turn out nobody's fools.

The seniors think they're better,
We know better than that,
You need to have a very big head
To fit in a very big hat.
We see them out at playtime,
They think they're so smart,
But we've made a very big bomb
And we'll blow them all apart...Oh!

Chorus

Dennis is a whizz-kid,
He deals with T.N.T.,
He makes Guy Fawkes look like a
shepherd
In the Nativity.
He's been through all the cellars,
This kid is not dumb.
And come next week we'll blow them all
Right to kingdom come...Oh!

Chorus

Tuesday is our day off,
We're going on a tour,
Down to the Houses of Parliament,
See how they rule the poor.
We'll learn all our lessons,
Each of us a gem,
And when we leave the school quite soon,
We're coming back for them...Oh!

Chorus

~ ~ ~ ~ ~

Nine Mates

Trevor is clever,
Stupid? Not ever.
But loveable...never.

Kelly is smelly,
Warts on her belly,
A clean girl? Not Kelly.

Leila? A failure,
Came from Westphalia
You need her? She'll mail yer.

Jimmy's a dimmy
He cannot swimmy,
No diving, how grimmy.

Penny's like Lenny,
They're two too many,
None like them, not any.

Lisa's a teaser,
Don't ever squeeze her,
There's nothing will please her.

Martha's like Arthur,
You'll never bath her,
Unless it's with Arthur.

Mates? Yes they're mates. Yes.
Should I be late, yes.
They will always wait. Yes!

My mates are my mates,
No-one like my mates,
And I love my nine mates.

~ ~ ~ ~ ~

Nasty Tomatoes

What really makes me quiver,
Is big, red, ripe tomatoes.
They make me blush and shiver,
All the way down to-ma-toes

It never is the small ones
That start my allergic trip,
It's always the big, red ones
That really give me the pip.

So if I ever see one
I just jump up to-ma-toes,
And run away to freedom
From those nasty tomatoes!

~ ~ ~ ~ ~

Nineteen Thirty-Nine

Upon the train the other day,
The guard had this to say:
"We'll be arriving right on time,
There will be no delay.
We'll get there at the scheduled time
Of Nineteen Thirty-Nine."
"Good grief!" I thought then to myself,
"We've travelled back in time!"
Imagine how I felt when I,
At last, the station saw,
Knowing that I would see the start
Of the Second World War.

~ ~ ~ ~ ~

Owl

The big old owl just said to me,
"Do you have any sweets?
I like it when you give me some,
I love those little treats."
I said that I was sorry that
There were no sweets today,
"Regretfully," I said to him,
"I gave them all away."
The owl, he simply looked at me,
And with no more to-do,
He narrowed his big eyes and said,
"You twit. To who? To who?"

~ ~ ~ ~ ~

Online Bird

Have you ever had a word with an online bird
Who never ever wants to meet,
For if you have a word with this online bird
You'll see he just prefers to tweet!

~ ~ ~ ~ ~

Oak Tree Making

A common deciduous forest tree,
Is the gnarled old oak,
And if your interest is forestry,
You'll be glad I spoke.

To make a deciduous forest tree,
As the said old oak,
You run along to an acorn tree
And with a stick – poke

Until an ingenuous acorn drops
Down upon the ground,
Making quite sure that the acorn stops
From rolling round.

Now take this ridiculous egg-like thing,
Sitting in its shell,
Give it a shake like a bell you ring
And with your nose - smell.

The smell is deliciously acorn-like,
Nutty in its way,
Reminding you of the things you like,
Pleasant, I should say.

Now with no maliciously hostile thoughts,
Plant it - add some rain,
And leave it alone for twenty years...
                    ...then begin again.

~ ~ ~ ~ ~

Old Hamster Jam

We used to own a hamster who was very old,
One day he died and we all cried,
No furry friend to hold.

We all were very sad that he had passed away,
But then I knew just what to do,
Upon that very day.

I took the little hamster, whom we all called Dan,
Removed his skin, and then placed him,
Inside a new saucepan.

Dan was tough to melt and we had to push and ram,
But very soon, upon the spoon,
We found ourselves with jam.

We then made some toast and spread the jam upon it,
We'd made our tea, but deary me,
That jam tasted horrid.

I took the jam and threw it out into the garden
But through the night, in the moonlight,
It began to harden.

Next day we all looked outside, sniffing with our noses,
And all around, all of the ground,
Was covered all with roses.

We blinked our eyes upon the view which swam and swam,
We would have bet, you'd always get
Tulips from hamster jam.

~ ~ ~ ~ ~

Origami

Origami, origami, origami, origami:
A word you can say fourfold.
There are thousands of things you can make from one sheet -
Its uses are so manifold!

~ ~ ~ ~ ~

Oxygen

Let's thank the stars that oxygen
Can't travel fast but goes quite slow,
For if it travelled faster then
You couldn't catch your breath, oh no!

~ ~ ~ ~ ~

Oh

There was a pink bird (name of Oh),
Who sunbathed all day (don't you know).
The heat it got higher
And Oh caught on fire,
Creating a pink flaming Oh.

~ ~ ~ ~ ~

Obstruction Clearing With My Cow

When driving on my cow one day
Down the motorway,
A flock of sheep was crossing
Then stood right in my way.
So I thought I'd make them rue
The day when they were born,
And then they seemed to shear themselves
When I blew the cow's horn.
MOOOO!

~ ~ ~ ~ ~

Old Aborigine

Old aborigine sitting by a tree,
Blowing down his didgeridoo,
When an old sheep farmer came and told him off,
Oh, what's an aborigine to do?

He can throw a boomerang at a Kangaroo,
Can make a noise just like a cockatoo,
But an old sheep farmer says he's not allowed
To blow down his didgeridoo.

~ ~ ~ ~ ~

P

Priscilla

There was a young girl called Priscilla,
Who thought that she was a gorilla,
She went to a park,
And just for a lark,
She married an ape called Godzilla.

~ ~ ~ ~ ~

Poem That Deserved To Be Eaten

This poem was scrumptious,
This poem was tasty.
Now no-one will read it.
Why was I so hasty?

~ ~ ~ ~ ~

Professor John

Professor John put his trousers on
The top of his head one day.
Then, with a cough, he took them off
And threw them far away.
I asked him to say why he'd thrown them away,
And then to my surprise,
He blushed bright red before he said
That the flies got in his eyes.

~ ~ ~ ~ ~

Piranha Boomerang

I once owned a piranha fish
That was bad in a nasty way
I stuck it to a boomerang
And I tried to throw it away
But as it left my fingertips
An awful thought came to fright me –
That pretty soon this dreadful fish
Would be coming back to bite me.

~ ~ ~ ~ ~

Plastic Duck

My plastic duck is filthy
I don't know where he's been
I put him in the bath with me
And now he's squeaky clean

~ ~ ~ ~ ~

Pity The Birds

Pity if you will, the stork,
Who has to be most shrewish,
He must be careful in his work
Because the baby's newish

Pity if you will, the cock
Whose crow could be much calmer,
For if he's calm at six o'clock
He will not wake the farmer.

Pity please the goose, I beg,
Who really wants a daughter,
For when she lays that monstrous egg
Her eyes begin to water.

Pity, if you will, the birds
Who cannot ever fly,
What's the use of being a bird
If you can't look down from high?

~ ~ ~ ~ ~

Pencil Song

Sung to the tune of Oh Carol *by Neil Sedaka*

Oh Pencil,
I am but a fool,
I can only use you
As a writing tool.
I can never use you like a crayon,
For colouring in,
I can only ever
Pencil you in.
Oh-oh…cha-cha-cha!

~ ~ ~ ~ ~

Poppycock

Did you know the word *mayday*
Comes from the French words *m'aider*?
And did you know that *poppycock*
Is from the Dutch word *pappercack*?

Now *m'aider* just means 'help me',
But you might not believe me,
When I say that in the Dutch tongue
Pappercack translates as 'soft dung'.

I need someone to help me
Before *I* call out, 'Mayday!'
Someone might throw some *pappercack*
If I write down this poppycock!

~ ~ ~ ~ ~

Potty Training

Dad said to me, only just now,
That we're going to train the potty.
I can't think why, and I can't think how,
He must be going dotty.

What do you train a potty to do?
To empty itself in the upstairs loo?
To clean itself without a to-do
And to rid the air of the smell of the poo?

Potty, potty, in the night,
Come over here it's all right.
All on your own, no need to worry,
I'm trained too, so there's no hurry.

Potty's underneath the bed,
I crack my whip, he shows his head,
I show the stick, oh clever potty,
He puts himself beneath my botty,

Ladies and Gents I do implore you
To watch this trick that I will show you.
They come to watch from north and south,
As I put my head in the potty's mouth.

Dad said to me, only just now,
That we're going to train the potty.
I can't think why, and I can't think how,
He *must* be going dotty.

~ ~ ~ ~ ~

Quizzical Poetical

1. Number the wives of Henry 8;
2. Battle of Hastings – give the date;
3. What would you put a helmet on?
4. What type of toy is Megatron?
5. Which planet's closest to the sun?
6. What animal was called Red Rum?
7. Which continent holds Timbuktu?
8. What's a bigger word for 'flu'?
9. What is the real name of Batman?
10. What would you say is a 'can-can'?
11. How many teeth are in your head?
12. What is the German word for 'bed'?
13. Who wrote *The Taming of the Shrew*?
14. Who invented the clerihew?
15. What would you find inside a hearse?
16. Was Florence Nightingale a nurse?
17. Which county is Southampton in?
18. Which painting has a great big grin?
19. What would do you if you rehearse?
20. Who is the writer of this verse?

And here's one I like the best:

21. Before they found Mount Everest,
Which mountain was higher than all the rest?

For answers you can take a look,
Find them at the end of this book,

~ ~ ~ ~ ~

Quintin's Scribble

Quintin is my brother,
He gurgles and he dribbles,
And when he talks it's very odd,
It's exactly like he scribbles,

Quintin's like no other,
He loves to munch and nibble,
But when he speaks, it's very strange,
It's as if he's speaking scribble.

Quintin's only twelve months,
He rarely has a quibble,
But when he does it's very cute,
When he tells us off in scribble.

~ ~ ~ ~ ~

Questions of Wasps

I never want to be a wasp,
Wasps are not for me
To sting and buzz? Make all that fuss?
I'd rather be a bee.

Bees make money with their honey,
Jars at fifty pee.
They build stout hives and live their lives
In quiet secrecy.

They always take good care of mum,
Giving her a comb.
They're good, sweet folk, who hate to smoke,
And take bright flowers home.

So when I see the bees at play,
I think of the wasp,
And ask a question that I'll mention:
What would you rather bee…

…or a wasp?

~ ~ ~ ~ ~

Question

I thought, when asked the question:
'What's the smallest British bird?'
The answer was the Finch.
Or so, that's what I'd heard.
But then, my friend, he said to me,
"There's one smaller than the Finch,
Which is the seldom heard
Lesser-spotted Halfinch."

But now I have a problem,
I think both of us are wrong.
Could you guess the smallest
By sight or by its song?
So I looked in my bird book,
On a shelf, sat in its nest,
And it said the smallest
Is, of course, the Goldcrest.

~ ~ ~ ~ ~

FACT: The goldcrest is so small it weighs
almost exactly the same as a 20p piece.

Question of the Future

A question once was put to me,
By a silly old friend of mine,
"What would you like said about you
In around two hundred years' time?"

Now this was not a question that I
Ever thought I'd have to engage,
But I said I'd like them to say,
"My word, he looks good for his age!"

~ ~ ~ ~ ~

Quink

Have you ever done a Quink?
It's not what you might think
It's when you close one eye very fast
Much quicker than a wink.

~ ~ ~ ~ ~

The Quantum Leap

Let me tell you about the Quantum Leap,
Let me tell you about his Ma.
For with the leap of the Quantum Leap,
His Ma always said he'd go far

~ ~ ~ ~ ~

Quiet and Still

I have a little furry dog,
Grandma went to buy it,
She said that I could name him,
And so I called him Quiet.

I have a plastic duck that floats,
With yellow back and bill,
Mum said to call him what I want,
And so I called him Still.

So when my Grandad shouts at me,
To keep Quiet and Still,
I say I've kept them all this time,
They're on the windowsill.

~ ~ ~ ~ ~

Qwertyuiop

Qwertyuiop is my top line
Asdfghjkl written next,
Zxcvbnm is my third line,
And I bet you're feeling vexed.

If **Qwertyuiop** is my first line,
Then **Asdfghjkl** so near by,
With **Zxcvbnm** being my last line,
What type of writer am I?

~ ~ ~ ~ ~

Answer:

R

Riddle

There are clues on every line to the eleven-letter answer

On the Isle of Lewis
They sing a Carroll
In the town of Borogove

They all snicker-snack
And drink their galumph
And dine out on Bander bird

They wock and jabber
They gimble and rath
And gyre to a slithy tove

While whiffling with sword
They tumtum the foe
And beamishly chortle joy

They frabjously play
Through the mimsy day
All frumious to the snatch

~ ~ ~ ~ ~

ANSWER: _ _ _ _ _ _ _ _ _ _ _

R.I.P. Stephen Morley

Old Stephen Morley
Woke up one day in bed
He thought that he was poorly
But he wasn't
He was dead

He looked so very peaceful
Lying there in death
But he never mentioned
He was only holding breath

+

**Here lies the body
Of poor old Stephen Morley
Who thought he was dead
When he was only poorly**

~ ~ ~ ~ ~

Reluctant Pig

Once, I owned a reluctant pig
I'd take it for a walk
I'd drag it all around the town
And try to sell pulled pork.

~ ~ ~ ~ ~

Racing Toilet

I knew a racing driver
Who owned a racing circuit
And as he didn't like it
He called it The Racing Toilet.

He used to drive me round it
For hours that wouldn't end
And as he was so boring
It would drive me around the bend.

~ ~ ~ ~ ~

Ratel

Do not have a fight with the ratel
For the end of it might well be fatal.
And stay far away if a cadger you be,
For this fierce honey badger won't lend you 10p.

~ ~ ~ ~ ~

Rebecca

There was a young girl called Rebecca,
Who thought that she was a woodpecker,
She went to a wood,
And pecked all she could,
Till the proper woodpeckers did deck her

~ ~ ~ ~ ~

Rocket

I bought my son a rocket,
He put it in his pocket,
But then his pants went up in flames
When he plugged it in a socket!

~ ~ ~ ~ ~

Roof Bird

There is a bird of little brain,
Stands on a roof in Berwick.
You may have heard that he's a crane,
That's why they call him Derrick.

~ ~ ~ ~ ~

Rossina

There was a young girl called Rossina,
Who drank down a pint of retsina,
She drank it in one,
Until it was done,
So please send her home if you've seen her.

~ ~ ~ ~ ~

S

Smethurst and the Tom-Toms

Caruthers said to Smethurst,
"I say, do you hear those drums?"
"Don't bother me," said Smethurst,
"I'm busy with my sums."
"But Smethurst," said Caruthers,
"I think that you should answer,
It could be Charles, Caruthers,
Your friend the ballroom dancer."
"Don't pester me," said Smethurst
"I cannot stop to tarry,
To chat with any Tom-Tom,
Dick-Dick or Harry-Harry."

~ ~ ~ ~ ~

So Hungry I Could...

Once, when I was starving
And half-way through a horse,
I realised I wasn't
As hungry as I thought.

~ ~ ~ ~ ~

Shenanigans

Remember John Shenanigan?
He married Mary Branagan,
But he had to begin again
When she ran off with Flanagan.

A selfish man was Flanagan,
He wanted just to tan again,
But he lost Mary Branagan
When she went off with Hannigan.

A sailing man was Hannigan,
Who sailed off in a galleon,
But silly Mary Branagan
Looked for another man again.

She then ran off with Lanagan,
Who beat her once – and then again!
A cruel man was Lanagan,
So Mary went and ran again.

Remember John Shenanigan?
Well Mary went right back again.
When they had thirteen child-er-en
She stopped with her Shenanigans!

~ ~ ~ ~ ~

Spider

The spider owned eight spindly legs,
And loved them all like heaven,
When he looked down upon the ground,
There lay one, leaving seven.

The spider took another drink
Of beer with whisky mix,
Then he looked down and what he found
Meant his legs numbered six.

The spider scratched a puzzled brow,
Whilst breathing, 'Saints Alive',
And from his crown a leg dropped down,
Which meant he'd only five.

The spider looked a tortured look,
This was not entertaining,
And nearly died when he espied
He had but four remaining.

Poor spider span a silken web,
He was bereft of answers.
He tried to tie his legs to him,
But only found three dancers.

The spider took a longer drink,
Not knowing what to do,
And through his haze he dropped his gaze
On legs which numbered two.

Sad spider downed a larger drink,
To help him try to stop it,
But on the floor there was one more,
Poor spider had to hop it.

The spider watched his last leg fall,
By now he couldn't care less,
And as he drank, his eyelids sank,
This spider now was legless.

~ ~ ~ ~ ~

Sizzling Sausages

Sizzling sausages,
I wonder where the porridge is?
We always eat our porridges
Before we have our sausages.

~ ~ ~ ~ ~

Serial Cuddler

I'm a serial cuddler, cuddler,
A serial cuddler – me!
    I cuddle my mam and I cuddle my gran
    And I cuddle my dad for free.

I'm a serial cuddler, cuddler,
A serial cuddler – me!
    I cuddle the dog when he's been for a jog
    And I cuddle my daft dog's flea.

I'm a serial cuddler, cuddler,
A serial cuddler – me!
    I cuddle the rat that's been caught by cat
    And I cuddle the back yard tree.

I'm a serial cuddler, cuddler,
A serial cuddler – me!
    I cuddle the horse and the cow, of course,
    And I cuddle the beans for tea.

I'm a serial cuddler, cuddler,
A serial cuddler – me!
    I cuddle the snails that live on the whales
    And I cuddle the great North Sea.

I'm a serial cuddler, cuddler,
A serial cuddler – me!
    I cuddle the earth with my arms round its girth
    That's the whole of the world, you see.

I'm a serial cuddler, cuddler,
A serial cuddler – me!
    I cuddle Mars then put my arms round the stars,
    And the universe cuddles me.

~ ~ ~ ~ ~

Stroked Spiders

A scientific fact, we're told,
By scientists, both young and old,
Is, if you can, a spider hold,
And stroke its back, it will go bald.

As grapes are grapes and figs are figs,
And geese are geese and pigs are pigs,
Stroked spiders never dance their jigs
Unless they're wearing brand new wigs.

~ ~ ~ ~ ~

Slimy Trails

When you walk down garden paths
You might see slimy trails,
And you ask yourself the question,
Are they made by slugs or snails?
But then they could have well been left
By birds with slimy tails,
Or kangaroos from billabongs,
Or tiny humpbacked whales?
Or could they be from outer space,
The residue from stars?
Or might they be the calling cards
Of aliens from Mars?
Or there again they might just be
The gossamer of moths,
A sickly trail deposited
By slimy toads with coughs.
But whatever it might be
Your defences harden,
For whoever left it there
Is eating up your garden.

~ ~ ~ ~ ~

Snake

There's a snake living at the bottom of the garden,
It's a very long snake.
It goes all the way to Baden-Baden.
(Or so they say, I do not know.)

I can see the snake from my bedroom window,
It's a very bright snake.
At night its body is a huge shiny glow.
(Or so they say, I do not know.)

I've heard this snake from my Grandmother's cottage,
It's a very loud snake.
And she lives down in old Pease Pottage
(Or so she says, I do not know.)

I smell this snake in our upstairs toilet,
It's a very foul snake.
But to give it a wash would only spoil it
(Or so they say, I do not know.)

The snake has crawlies running all over it,
It's a very ill snake.
These crawlies are noisy and always cover it.
(Or so they say, I do not know.)

I rode on this snake, it was only yesterday,
It's a very big snake.
My dad said it was the Great Chertsey Motorway.
(Or so he said, I don't think he knows.)

~ ~ ~ ~ ~

T

T

Once upon a time back in school,
My old teacher pointed at me,
And asked me to think of something
That began with the letter 'T'.
She wanted to know a subject
At which I was *not* very good,
But I just stared and looked at her
As if I had not understood.
Most of the kids started laughing,
Some of the others were yelling,
So, to shut them up I answered
"My worst thing of all - is 'Spelling'."

~ ~ ~ ~ ~

Time Traveller

When I met him at the station,
He said he was a traveller in time.
When I asked him what he meant, he said:
"I just travelled in the ten past nine."

~ ~ ~ ~ ~

Tea is for Salad

Radishes, radishes,
I wonder where the radish is?
Can't wait to get my gnashers in,
When I find those radishes.

Lettuces, lettuces,
I wonder where the lettuce is?
Can't wait to take my lettuce in,
If the lettuce lets us in.

Cucumber, Cucumber,
All hail and praise the cucumber.
It's in the fridge that cucumber
It should be a cool-cumber.

Celery, celery,
Is he in the cellar he?
The downstairs room is cellar-y,
It's where I keep the celery.

Salad tea salad tea,
How I love a salad tea.
Radish, lettuce, cool-cumber,
And don't forget the celery!

~ ~ ~ ~ ~

Tongue Twister

Sheila sells her shiny shrines
                    in her shiny shrine shop
It's in the shiny shrine shop
                    where Sheila sells her shrines
If Sheila wants to sell more shrines
                    in the shiny shrine shop
Where should shop-keep Sheila
                    show her shiny shrine signs?

~ ~ ~ ~ ~

Trolls

Trolls live in holes and stick you with poles,
        If you live by a northern sea,
But cats lie on mats and eat nasty rats,
        And sound a lot nicer to me.

Trolls have no souls and eat new-born foals,
        That happen to be in the way,
But dogs play with frogs that hide under logs,
        And that's a lot nicer I'd say.

Trolls don't play bowls, write nicely on scrolls,
        Or smile at the nice things you say.
They growl and they're foul, and at night they howl,
        I think that we're nicer...okay?

~ ~ ~ ~ ~

Things I Have Seen

I've seen bat caves in Bolivia
And voles in Viet Nam
A starving horse in Hungary
Deep holes in Pakistan

I fought cats in Costa Rica
Ate bees in old Thailand
Watched sunsets in America
Sailed seas round Ireland

I've drunk tea inside a tee-pee,
In Belarus I danced
And then one day I watched some boys
Go tease a frog in France

I've seen things I cannot talk of
Events you'd not believe
Like grimalkins on fiery heaths
Things you could not conceive

Vampires in Transylvania
And mermaids in New York
Devils in dark Tasmania
Who giggle when they talk

A cockatrice in Latvia
A minotaur in Greece
Piranha fish in Liverpool
Who ate a scaly beast

I have seen the Niagara Falls
Completely freeze one night
And I have seen brave heroes
Fight darkness till it's light

But of all those many wonders
Of all those mystic scenes
There's one thing I have yet to see –
You - finishing your greens

~ ~ ~ ~ ~

T-H Words

Unlucky things are Spelling birds
Constantly attacked by T-H words
They fend off words like 'This' and 'There'
But quite often get caught unaware
Even if they sit there humming
They always fail to see 'That' coming.

~ ~ ~ ~ ~

Tell Us A Story Mammy

Tell us a story Mammy,
Tell to us a tale,
Tell us all about the big white whale.
Was he a monster Mammy
With a big tail?
Tell us Mammy all about the big white whale.

Tell us a story Mammy,
Tell us of the air,
Tell us all about the things up there.
Are they right scary Mammy
Covered with hair?
Tell us Mammy all about the things up there.

Tell us a story Mammy,
Tell us of the sea,
Tell us all about what we might see.
Is it right awful Mammy
Dark as can be?
Tell us Mammy all about what we might see.

Tell us a story Mammy,
Tell to us a yarn,
Tell us all about the socks you darn.
Are they right smelly Mammy,
Knitted with yarn?
Tell us Mammy all about the socks you darn.

Tell us a story Mammy,
You can make it so,

Tell us all about where we might go.
Will we travel far Mammy,
Do you not know?
Tell us Mammy all about where we might go.

Tell us a story Mammy,
Tell of things to come,
Tell us all about what we'll become.
Will we be happy Mammy,
Will we be glum?
Tell us all about it Mammy,
Tell us all about it Mammy,
Please tell us about it Mammy,
Tell us Mammy all about what we'll become.

~ ~ ~ ~ ~

Tomorrow Man

There was a young man from tomorrow,
Who came back in order to borrow,
Some loot for a bet,
On a race not run yet,
By a horse that would win on the morrow

~ ~ ~ ~ ~

U

Uncle

My uncle was killed when he swallowed his tuba,
It was a ghastly sight to see.
We buried him then on the south side of Cuba,
The funeral was very low key.

~ ~ ~ ~ ~

Universe is Chocolate

The universe is chocolate,
There's sweets among the stars,
Where you'll find treats so great to eat,
Like *Galaxy* and *Mars*.

You have *Revels* in a *Starburst*
And *Picnic* all the day,
When you take a *Flying Saucer*
Along the *Milky Way*.

~ ~ ~ ~ ~

Uranusquake

If there's an earthquake on Uranus,
What would it be called?
Would it be a *Uranusquake*?
I think we should be told.

~ ~ ~ ~ ~

Ugandan Girl

There was a young girl from Uganda,
Who decided her geese should be blander.
She worked hard all day
Taking sweetness away,
Till she fell in love with a gander.

~ ~ ~ ~ ~

Umbrella

I have in my hands an old umbrella
I bought it from a little old feller,
It's black on the outside but within coloured yeller,
She's my pride and joy and I'm never gonna sell 'er.

~ ~ ~ ~ ~

Uncle Dennis

My uncle Dennis
Was killed playing tennis
When he fell after slipping on ice.
I would like to say, when we sent him away,
His service was all very nice.

~ ~ ~ ~ ~

U and Me and an Ass

When I passed your room,
I heard you assume,
You thought you could see
The donkey in me.
I said, "I presume,
If you so assume,
An ASS you will see
Made of U and ME."

~ ~ ~ ~ ~

Ursula

Now Ursula was a young girl
Who wanted to spin and to twirl,
She turned so far round,
That she entered the ground,
Now Ursula cannot unfurl.

~ ~ ~ ~ ~

Universe

If I wrote two poems
About a couple of suns,
This might well be called
A duo verse.
But if I write one poem
About every sun there is,
This might well be called
A universe.

(Please note that this poem only has one verse.)

~ ~ ~ ~ ~

Very Young Poet's Dilemma

The cat sat on the mat...?
What on earth is there that rhymes with that...?

~ ~ ~ ~ ~

Vegetarian's Search

Cabbages, cabbages,
I wonder where the cabbage is?
I've looked all round and in between,
Have you seen my delicious greens?

Potatoes, potatoes,
Where did they go, those potatoes?
I've now sent out potato spies,
I hope they use potato eyes.

Onions, onions,
I had some odd-shaped funny ones.
They disappeared, went out to hide,
You won't believe how much I've cried.

All my veg, all my veg,
I have lost my lovely veg.
I've only found a single bean:
A vegetarian has-been!

~ ~ ~ ~ ~

Vain Money Waster

There was a young lady so vain,
She would never be seen in the rain,
And such was her haste
That she tended to waste
All her money which went down the drain.

~ ~ ~ ~ ~

Very Deep Sea

I always love the ocean, me,
I love to take the plunge,
But how much deeper would it be,
If it lacked every sponge?

~ ~ ~ ~ ~

Very Weird Friends

I have friends that are weird, friends that are feared,
And there are those I think are rather cool.
There are some of them quite wise,
Others, nutters in disguise,
We're pretty much an ordinary school:

Frances goes to dances where she prances,
And Bunny likes to hop when at the bop.
Then Arthur makes advances
On anyone he fancies,
Until the dance is over then he'll stop.

Milly looks at Billy then is silly.
She'd like to take him back to her Grandma's,
They'd turn him in a jiffy
Straight into piccalilli
Then take him off to market in jam jars.

Grace is pulling faces at the races,
She's backed the horse she first saw on the course.
But it's not really funny
As she loses her money
And they have to take her off the course by force.

Jenny May Kilkenny stares at Benny
Who does the most outrageous belly flops.
So, then Jenny asks him why
He thinks he's a butterfly
And Benny says it's lovely when it stops.

Johnny says to Connie, "You look bonny",
He says it in the most convincing way.
It is then she takes command

Grabbing his fat, sweaty hand,
And now you see them wrestling every day.

Polly says, "Oh golly, I'm so jolly!
I'm such a happy person all the time."
But then she starts to hurry
Because there is a worry
That to be jolly must be thought a crime.

Denny has so many friends like Lenny.
Who's annoying and spoiling for a fight.
So when they go out for lunch
Lenny gets a rabbit punch,
Now Lenny knows that fighting isn't right.

Billy is a very silly Billy,
Sometimes you really don't know where to look.
There are days when he's a dog,
Then he's hopping like a frog,
Then lays an egg as if he is a duck.

Trevor cannot ever look at Heather,
It seems that he has fallen quite in love.
If she smiles at him a bit,
It's as if he has been hit
By a massive fist inside a boxing glove.

So, if all your friends drive you round the bend,
Remember it's the same inside a zoo.
From the weird ones to the meek,
Every creature is unique,
We're all just human beings through and through.

~ ~ ~ ~ ~

Vegetable Men

They told me of the vegetable men,
Of how they march in November,
When the nights are as crisp as lettuce
And carrots fresh from the ground.

They told me of their vegetable legs,
Of how they ran to remember
Where they had left their vegetable heads
And bellies, cabbagey round.

They told me if you got in the way
Of the vegetables in November,
They'd think of you as one of their own,
And take you down underground.

Down to where all the vegetable men
Weather the cold of December,
And hope that they will rise up again,
Once more when Spring comes around.

~ ~ ~ ~ ~

Viking

Viking, Viking, oh Viking, vy?
Vy did you let the Qveen fly so high?
She flew on a Vensday and vent through the sky,
Viking, Viking, oh Viking, vy?

Viking, Viking, vot have you done?
Vy did you let Qveen fly to the sun?
She flew so very close she began to fry,
Viking, Viking, oh Viking, vy?

Viking, Viking, ver did she go?
She seemed to float up oh so slow.
Then ve saw her melt and vriggling die,
Viking, Viking oh Viking, vy?

Viking, Viking? You gave her vings,
Because she drives you crazy ven she sings,
Now she is a screech bird deafening you and I,
Viking, Viking, oh Viking, vy?

~ ~ ~ ~ ~

Voice of the Sharpening Song

My father likes to sing along
When he's sharpening things.
He calls it his Sharpening Song,
Which he most loudly sings.
What it's about I do not know,
And I don't mean to carp,
'Cos I can't bear to listen, for
His voice is always sharp.

~ ~ ~ ~ ~

Vow Of The Gingerbread Man

Caught with his hands inside the biscuit tin,
The gingerbread man coughed,
And promised he'd never do it again,
Well...
...he won't with his hands bitten off...
...will he?

~ ~ ~ ~ ~

W

William Shakespeare

William Shakespeare
Would sometimes appear
As an actor upon the Globe stage,
But his acting was not all the rage.

~ ~ ~ ~ ~

Winner of the Naughty Limerick Competition

Tee-tumpity tumpity tum
Tee-tumpity tumpity tum
Tee-tumpity tee
Tee-tumpity tee
Tee-tumpity tumpity bum

Young poets are welcome to create their own naughty limerick
which they think will be better than this winner of the competition.

~ ~ ~ ~ ~

When My Voice Broke

When my voice broke...

        ...I was taking part...

In a concert...

        ...at the Sacred Heart…

I was to be...

        ...one of the three kings...

One of the three...

        ...soloists that sings…

When my voice broke...

        ...I was badly shocked...

The other kings...

        ...broadly smiled and mocked...

My voice it cracked...

        ...like an old jam jar...

Miserable un...

        …happy Balthazar...

~ ~ ~ ~ ~

Why, Oh – Why, Oh

Why, oh – why, oh,
Do I do those things, oh,
That they tell me are a no-no?

Why, oh – why, oh,
When I write out 'why, oh – why, oh',
Does it spell out the word 'yo-yo'?

~ ~ ~ ~ ~

Why I Hate Sourdough Toast

They say that sourdough's good for you,
They say the whole world knows,
But when you melt the butter on,
It drips through on your toes.

They tell me sourdough's healthy,
As good as crisp fresh greens,
But when you melt the butter on,
It drips down on your jeans.

They tell me sourdough's trendy,
So chic and such a treat,
But when you melt the butter on,
It drips upon your feet.

They brag that sourdough's different,
And goes so well with eggs,
But when you melt the butter on,
It drips along your legs.

They say sourdough's traditional,
Though you must be alert,
But when you melt the butter on,
It drips through on your shirt.

Sourdough bread's the best there is,
So everyone agrees,
But when you melt the butter on,
It ends up on your knees.

So if you don't want butter,
Spoiling all your clothes,
Eat rye bread, wheatgerm anything
But sourdough toasted loaves.

~ ~ ~ ~ ~

William Archibald Spooner

William Archibald Spooner
Was an old Oxford don,
Whose words were often quite mixed up,
Put simply, they were wrong.
A student said, "It seems to be
A *plush folly* what you do."
And that's the reason why he flushed
The parrot down the loo.

~ ~ ~ ~ ~

Whale Warning

Just the other day as I was walking down the road,
I met a whale who told me he was going to explode.
So I ran along the street telling those I know:
"There is no doubt about it,
I'll shout it and I'll spout it,
Get yourselves inside because this whale is going to
blow!"

~ ~ ~ ~ ~

Who Will Rid Me Of This Turbulent Beast?

"Who will rid me of this turbulent beast?"
The King demanded to know.
He then looked round at his truculent priest
Who blushed, his nose aglow.

"I do not really know sire,"
The priest began to speak,
"I banished it to hell sire,
But it came back last week."

"Who will rid me of this turbulent beast?"
The King requested once more,
He looked at his baker, covered in yeast,
Who edged towards the door.

"I cannot really tell sire,"
The baker then did say,
"We put it in the fire, sire,
But it came back today."

"Who will rid me of this turbulent beast?"
The King requested again,
He looked at his son who sat at the feast,
Whose name was Prince Gawain.

"I don't think I can say, Dad,
I don't think I know how,
We locked it in the barn, Dad,
It ate a horse and cow."

176

"Who will rid me of this turbulent beast?"
The King now did implore,
He then looked upon the actual beast,
Which lay upon the floor.

"I don't think you like me King,"
The beast sulked from below,
"I think you're a silly King,
You're not much fun, you know.

So I ate your old horse, King,
What's a poor beast to do?
Locking me in a barn, King,
I could have caught the 'flu.

How would you like the fire, King,
If it happened to you?
And hell is not so nice, King
It's worse than in the zoo.

So now I'm going home, King,
Can't think what I did wrong,
You'll soon find you'll miss me, King,
When all the fun is gone."

~

"Who will now find me my turbulent beast?"
The King did beg his court,
"It's been a month now since all the fun ceased
The beast must now be caught."

"We've searched all through the land, King,
We've looked from shore to shore,
The beast has disappeared, King."
...And it was seen no more.

Once there was a lonely king,
Who died before he should,
He missed the fun the beast would bring,
Like the beast said he would.

~ ~ ~ ~ ~

Witchiest Witch

Which witch there was the witchiest witch?
Not one of the witches knew.
They found out when the witchiest witch
Turned the others into stew.

Which stew there was the stewiest stew?
Only the stewiest knew.
They all knew when the stewiest stew
Ate the rest and grew and grew.

Witchiest witch met stew in a ditch
And ate it all with a spoon.
Witch now sits all alone in the ditch,
Groaning underneath the moon.

~ ~ ~ ~ ~

X

Xmas

Please don't think me a failure,
An ass or a fool or a peasant,
But Xmas past is not for me,
I prefer a Xmas present.

~ ~ ~ ~ ~

Xara's Bomb

I'm going to make a Bomb,
That's what I'll call the dress
I will design,
In record time,
In order to impress.

And when I put it on,
The bomb and I will BOOM!
We'll stun the Prom
When me and Bomb
Explode into that room!

~ ~ ~ ~ ~

X's = Kisses

Around about one Xmas-time,
An X came out to walk.
Upon his way he met a friend,
And they began to talk.

"What brings you here?" the first X said,
"Could it be for the fun?
Or have you come to stroll around
Beneath the setting sun?"

The second X said, "Not at all,
It's you I've come to seek,
For do you know that we've not met
For longer than a week?

Why is it you've forsaken me?
You know I love you so,
Why did you ever move away,
Why ever did you go?"

The first X looked around about,
And blushing looked away
Towards the shining meadow grass,
And thought just what to say.

"I love you too," he said at last,
"I'll love you ever more,
But I could never marry you,
For I'll be ever poor."

The second X said, "Worry not,
It's you that I have missed,
Not gold or wealth or riches..."
                    ...and so the X's XXXXed.

~ ~ ~ ~ ~

X

X is a Roman numeral,
I use it now and then,
Sometimes it helps me mark the spot,
Sometimes it equals ten.
Sometimes it shows me when I'm wrong,
Sometimes it crosses out
A poem that I'm working on
Which I just can't work out.
Sometimes it helps me multiply,
Sometimes it's just a kiss
Placed at the bottom of a card
Sent to the ones I miss.

~ ~ ~ ~ ~ ~

X-Ray

I used to know a man whose name was Ray,
Who broke his leg and so they X-rayed Ray.
They told him when would be his X-ray day,
But just before, poor Ray, he passed away.
We think about poor Ray from day to day,
And when we do, we speak about ex-Ray.

~ ~ ~ ~ ~

Xebec

A xebec was an old sailing ship
That was once sailed by old corsairs
Now sailors are known to use coarse words
But not as coarse as old corsairs

~ ~ ~ ~ ~

Xebras

Xebras are an oddity,
A strange-ish kind of horse.
Their stripes they don't go up and down,
In fact, the black lines cross.
If one walks in front of you,
Please start your applausing,
For what you see ahead of you,
Is a Xebra Crossing.

~ ~ ~ ~ ~

Xylocarp

The xylocarp is a wild nutty fruit,
That likes to shout and harp on
About the fact that its name tags
Have all got Xylocarp on.

~ ~ ~ ~ ~

Xylophone

Xylophone, Xylophone,
A useless set of plates,
There's never anyone at home,
When I ring up my mates.

Xylophone, Xylophone,
You really make me sick,
So now I'll start to make you groan,
I'll hit you with this stick.

Xylophone, Xylophone,
Oh what a lovely noise,
You're a different kind of phone,
Can't wait to ring the boys.

~ ~ ~ ~ ~

Y

Y?

Of all the alphabet letters
I'm friends with twenty-five.
"Why only twenty-five?" you ask,
I'm afraid I don't know why.

~ ~ ~ ~ ~

Yawn

The yawn is a terrible sneak-up thing,
It creeps up without warning,
Just when the school bell starts to ring,
You suddenly find you're yawning.

The yawn is a horrible crafty wain,
Don't ever ask for warning,
For when the teacher calls your name,
You answer, 'Here,' while yawning.

The Yawn isn't sensible nor admired,
For leaving out its warning,
'Cos when you're asked if you are tired
You just can't stop your yawning.

The Yawn means trouble for everyone,
One and all without warning,
For though we've slept twelve hours plus one,
We never can stop yawning.

~ ~ ~ ~ ~

Yodelling

If   I   yodel,
   only   could

How   I   be,
   happy   would

I'd   the
   be   best,

Beat   the
   all   rest

Of   yodelling   -tern-   -ty!
   the   fra-   -i-

~ ~ ~ ~ ~

Yoobub

The Yoobub is a thingumybob,
A thingumybob with snoo,
The Yoobub is a whatsumycall
That should be in a zoo.

The Yoobub is a howdoyousay,
A howdoyousay with snay,
The Yoobub is a whichumything
That stays out night and day.

The Youbub is a whatyummysmell.
A whatyummysmell with snork,
The Yoobub is a knowwhatImean,
That eats with knife and fork.

The Yoobub is a whatsitawhat,
A whatsitawhat with sweak,
The Yoobub is a whatsthatagain,
That still declines to speak.

The Yoobub is a seenembefore,
A seenembefore with splance.
The Yoobub is a flippertyflap,
That loves to flirt and dance.

The Yoobub is a howdoyoudo,
A howdoyoudo with splack,
The Yoobub is a whereishenow,
I hope that he comes back.

~ ~ ~ ~ ~

You Know It Makes Sense

Come down from that ladder and eat up your tea,
If you break your both legs don't come running to me.

Don't play with those scissors, don't make me shout it,
If you cut off your tongue don't tell me about it.

Don't mess with that needle, it's sharp don't you see,
If you poke out your eyes don't come looking for me.

Don't climb, play or meddle, you're making me tense,
You know what I'm saying...
                              ...you know it makes sense.

~ ~ ~ ~ ~

Younger

The man said to me, "Here's a photograph,
It's of me when I was younger."
I said, "But every photograph of you,
Is of you when you were younger."

~ ~ ~ ~ ~

Yakety Yak

(With apologies to the 1950's rock and roll band, The Coasters)

The Yakety yak came back to town,
Still dressed in her wedding gown,
She'd only gone and run away
From her bridegroom that very day.

Yakety yak – don't talk back

She gathered all the people round,
She made them sit there on the ground,
And then she started to convey
The reasons why she ran away.

Yakety yak – don't talk back

Her bridegroom was a lovely yak,
Who would insist on talking back,
She'd thought that he would fit the bill,
But he would answer back at will.

Yakety yak – don't talk back

She knew she could not live with this,
It could not end in married bliss,
And so she let the marriage fail,
And now she bores them with the tale.

Yakety yak – don't talk back

So if you ever meet a yak,
Who won't allow you to talk back,
Then you must run without delay,
Or you won't ever get away.

> *Yakety yak – Yakety yak*
> *Yakety yak – Yakety yak*
> *Yakety yak – Yakety yak*
> *Yakety yak – Yakety yak*

~ ~ ~ ~ ~

Yelp

There once was a thing called a Yelp,
Which lived by the sea in the kelp.
If it once got into trouble
It jumped at the double,
And we'd all hear the Yelp yelping, "Help!"

~ ~ ~ ~ ~

Yesterday

(With apologies to The Beatles)

Yesterday,
All my troubles were a mile away,
I wrote a song about it, then today,
The song had gone and run away.

Suddenly,
I searched everywhere that it could be,
Even beneath the old settee,
Why has this song done this to me?

Where it had to go,
I don't know,
I cannot say.
It took all day long, my new song,
Called Yesterday.

~ ~ ~ ~ ~

Z

Zealous Photographer

He went to take a photograph
Of a massive crocodile,
Whose jaws began to open wide…
In the biggest…ever…smile.

And so he moved much closer to
That gargantuan reptile,
While looking through the camera lens…
And the croc…maintained…its smile.

Then as he poked his head inside,
Past the rows of teeth and smile,
A glint appeared within its eye…
A snap-happy…croc…o…dile!

~ ~ ~ ~ ~

Zanzi Bar

I once went to visit a Zanzi bar,
Where they served specialist zanzis.
A splash of the zans would give it its ziz
Much better by far than cranberries.

~ ~ ~ ~ ~

Zig-Zag

Zig-zag, zig-zag, oh zig-zag,
Why do you never see,
It is so much easier
To go from **A** to **B**?

Why do you ever need to
Go via letter **C**,
Then stop off at **D**, **E**, **F**,
Or visit letter **G**?

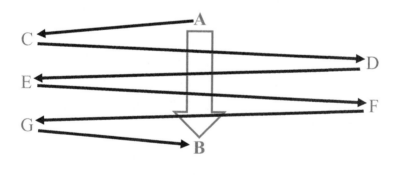

~ ~ ~ ~ ~

Zoomorphic Me

I really am zoomorphic,
I change without a care.
One minute I'm the same old me,
The next, I am a bear.

And if the mood should take me,
Standing in a station,
Instead of getting on the train –
I'm in hibernation.

And when at last I wake up,
And feel I need to jog,
I simply change myself again
Into a greyhound dog.

It's fun being zoomorphic.
When I've just had a bath,
I'll look into the mirror and
A hippo makes me laugh.

Zoomorphic me is happy,
I change myself to suit,
If I can't reach the trees then a
Giraffe will pick the fruit.

If I should meet a person
Who bores me fit to snore,
I simply turn into a pig,
And show him who's a boar.

And should I find a bully,
Who sneers with every breath,
Into a tiger I will turn
And scare him half to death.

Of course, I am endangered,
The last one of my kind,
But lots of us are changeable,
It's just a state of mind.

~ ~ ~ ~ ~

Zappy

My baby brother Zappy,
Is the cutest little chappie
Especially when he's had enough to eat
And when it all comes out
You should hear him shout
He's the greatest happy-clappy Zappy in a
nappy
You'd ever want to meet!

~ ~ ~ ~ ~

Zara

There once was a woman called Zara,
Who wore an expensive tiara.
Round the town she'd be seen,
Saying she was the Queen,
Which made all the shopkeepers bar her.

~ ~ ~ ~ ~

Zebu

The zebu is a hump-backed cow
That lives in farthest India.
The hump-back stops it falling down
When India gets windier.

~ ~ ~ ~ ~

Zeppelin

Why did they build it oh so large,
That huge and monstrous Zeppelin?
They built it massive, this cigar,
So they could get the people in.
And once inside this grand cigar,
You all can ride and travel in
Plush comfort like a Rolls Royce car,
Secure within the Zeppelin.
But when you look at this cigar,
Don't ever put a light to it,
You really won't get very far,
If once you have ignited it.

~ ~ ~ ~ ~

Zed to Ay

Zed is always left aside, right to the very end,
Wy is never far behind – Wy is Zed's only friend.
Ekks is very, very nice, signed with a loving kiss,
Double Yoo is put down twice, in case the first you miss.
Vee comes after single Yoo, before the Double, too,
Yoo is all alone you know and sobs the whole night through.
Tee is happy all the day and laughs Tee-hee, tee-hee,
Ess does not know what to say but knows what she can see.
Arr is gasping out with pain, it's hot under his feet,
Kyew is hiding from the rain, his tail beneath his seat.
Pee is hopping up and down, bursting with the strain,
Ohh looks on and bears a frown, he really is quite vain.
Enn is very dignified, there's nothing he derides,
Emm is ever mystified, but she can see both sides.
Ell is nearly always hot, from lying underground,
Kay just loves to trot and trot, then jump in one long bound.
Jay is very insular, making her real snotty,
Aye sees all there is to see, which makes her rather dotty.
Aitch just loves to sing and sing, the others block their ears
Gee cannot believe a thing he sees or smells or hears,
Eff is rather frightening, she screams and swears and sneers,
Eee is like greased lightning and runs away in tears.
Dee has put on too much weight, which makes him stretch his
back,
See is never ever late, in case she gets the sack.
Bee has got a double chin, which he thinks is a crime,
But Ay just loves to start it all, that's why she hates this
rhyme.

~ ~ ~ ~ ~

THE END   *…or is it…?*

PS...

MOSQUITO

Written by Max Morley when aged 9

The mosquito is a horrible creature,
Sucking blood is its main feature.
If there's a lump where your skin is pink,
That means the mosquito has had a drink.

The mosquito is a horrible creature,
Sucking blood is its main feature
At night it will come out to meet ya,
Put on some spray or it'll eat ya!

~ ~ ~ ~ ~

Quizzical Poetical Answers

1. Six
2. 1066
3. Your head
4. A Transformer
5. Mercury
6. A (race) horse
7. Africa
8. Influenza
9. Bruce Wayne
10. A dance
11. 32
12. Bett
13. William Shakespeare
14. Edmund Clerihew Bentley
15. A coffin
16. Yes
17. Hampshire
18. *The Laughing Cavalier*
19. Prepare something
20. See the front cover
21. Mount Everest (of course!)

EGGS - DELIBERATE MISTAKE:
Kippers can't swim either!

Also Available from Amazon

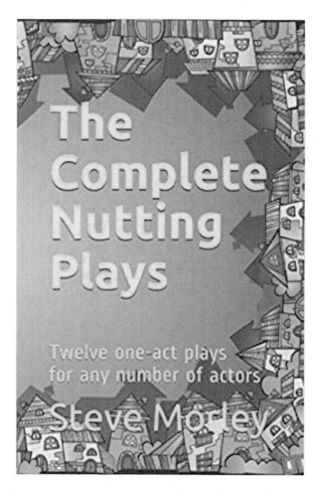

Nutting is a town where everybody lives ordinary lives in an extraordinary way, and where everyone who lives there is known as a Nutter.

Printed in Great Britain
by Amazon